I0626170

Over Her Knee, Denied By Her, &
In Her Care
…plus the bonus erotic short story
"Tape"

# Becoming
# Hers
# Trilogy Set

## SHOSHANNA EVERS

Dedicated to my kinky readers.

# CONTENTS

# ACKNOWLEDGMENTS

Thank you to my cover designer Rob Sturtz, for designing the Becoming Hers Series covers. Thank you to contemporary romance author Heather Thurmeier, erotic romance authors Anh Leod and Charlotte Stein, and romance reader extraordinaire Kelly Ludwig for editing this series, back when it was the Dominatrix Fantasy Trilogy. Your feedback has been invaluable.

Thank you to erotic romance author Elizabeth Thorne for editing the short story *Tape. Tape* is also published in the anthology Felt Tips, edited by Harlequin Spice and MIRA author Tiffany Reisz.

And thank you to my readers. You are the reason I write, and I love you all. If you enjoyed this book, it would be wonderful if you could leave a review on the site where you purchased it. I look forward to hearing what you think!

Please stay in touch and connect with me on Twitter, Facebook, and via my newsletter if you haven't already!

BECOMING HERS SERIES

OVER
HER KNEE

Novella 1

New York Times Bestselling Author

Shoshanna
EVERS

# OVER HER KNEE: NOVELLA 1

Blake Claren straightened the ridiculous white hat all of the waiters at the '50s-themed diner had to wear and glanced again at the beautiful, dark-haired woman sitting in the booth. He'd watched as she walked decisively though the jingling front door, was offered a seat at the counter (the usual protocol for single diners, to save space during the heavy lunch hour rush) and while Blake hadn't overheard her response to the hostess, it had earned her a seat at the gleaming four-top.

"You better get over there," the hostess advised under her breath. "She means business."

Blake laughed but he knew exactly what his friend meant. The woman had already pulled out her PDA and an e-reader and was doing something important-looking with them. She had a way about her, as if anything she took the time to do had to be important.

"Fuck," Blake whispered under his breath. He could already tell this woman wasn't going to take his stupid restaurant-required spiel lightly.

*Just go over there. It's not like she's going to bite you.* Heat rushed through his face, since getting love-bites was one of his favorite things.

"Good afternoon, ma'am," he said as he ambled over to her table. "Welcome to the '50s and to some darn good food." He grimaced inwardly at the canned line, hoping it didn't show on his face.

*She might not bite, but I deserve to be bitten for actually saying this stuff.*

The woman set her electronic devices on the table and looked up at him, her lipsticked lips smiling. Blake could tell right away this woman smiled when she was annoyed. It shouldn't have, but it scared him in the same exhilarating way rollercoasters scared him—that gorgeous, straight-toothed smile that seemed to say *"Why should I deign to respond to you?"*

And just like with a rollercoaster, he was ready for a ride.

"I'm sorry to interrupt you, ma'am," he said hastily. "Are you ready to order? Do you want me to come back, ma'am?"

Saying ma'am twice in one breath was a bit much even for him, but something about her commanding presence seemed to require it. Blake had the uncomfortable, butterflies-in-the-stomach sensation that he'd upset her, or that he was in trouble or something, even though the woman hadn't said a word. It was a feeling he'd chased in the past—because it turned him on.

"Diet Coke, please," the woman said.

"Yes ma'am."

Blake quickly turned to go fetch her soda. Her polite words surprised him. He'd half-expected her to give him a direct order, perhaps kick him under the table with one of those high-heeled black boots she wore with her fitted business suit.

His cock jerked to half-mast at this thought, thankfully hidden beneath his trousers and white apron. It shouldn't turn him on to imagine himself at a woman's mercy, but it did. It always did. *Stop thinking like that.*

But Blake couldn't help himself. A hot, strong woman telling him what to do, letting him serve her however she saw fit, was such a turn-on. *Damn it.* There'd be no hiding his erection now. He took a few deep breaths and focused on baseball, holding the icy glass, now slippery with condensation in his hand.

It took several moments before his body was under control again and he was able to give the woman her drink.

"Here you go," he said cheerfully, fully aware that his manager was always watching, making sure the waiters stuck to the proper feel of the diner.

"Why thank you," the woman replied, the cool smile on her lips bringing heat to Blake's cheeks. "That only took you ten times as long as it should have."

Usually attitude like that from a customer brought up his defensiveness and made him want to spit in her food—not that he'd ever have dared, since he needed this job to pay his rent. But for reasons quite unclear to him, the woman's criticism only spurred his desire to serve her better.

"I'm sorry ma'am," he said. "Extremely sorry. Have you decided what you'd like to order?"

But she'd already picked up her PDA and e-reader and was back to doing whatever it was she'd decided to spend her lunch hour working on. She looked up at him as if amazed he was still there.

"Cobb salad, dressing on the side, please."

"Yes ma'am." He put the order in and ran into his floor manager at the counter, a burly older man with a belly that even the white apron couldn't hide.

"Come on kiddo, go do your thing. You can't just pick and choose which customers to entertain."

"She won't like it," Blake said. "I can tell."

"And I won't like it if you don't," he said, handing him a plate of salad. "She came in here for a reason, right?"

Blake sighed and walked back to the woman's booth, feeling as if he were heading to his own execution. The woman was deep into whatever it was she was working on.

"Ma'am? I'm sorry to interrupt you." He set her salad onto the table in front of her, dressing on the side as per her request.

The woman set down her devices slowly, one long-nailed hand smoothing her dark hair away from her face. Blake looked at her fingers, fascinated by the glossy burgundy polish. Her right hand, however, had nails clipped short, though still glossy and dark. Only the left hand had long, dangerous-looking fingernails.

Her smile—that cool, dismissing smile—set his heart racing again. "Blake," she said, reading his name off his nametag. "You've had to apologize to me numerous times."

"I'm sorry, ma'am," he said, then bit his lip. That was probably the last thing she'd want to hear.

"Perhaps," she said, "you'd be better off if you focused on serving me properly instead of in such a way that necessitated apology."

"Yes, ma'am."

"And what is the interruption for this time?"

"Um, this may seem like a stupid question, but what is your favorite animal?"

"A dog," she replied. Her expression had changed to one of amusement, as if she were tolerating his behavior only because she knew he'd be severely punished for it the more he dug himself into a hole.

*No, stop thinking like that. You can't afford to get a hard-on in front of this woman.*

Blake picked up the plastic ketchup container off the table and a small plate, and carefully drew a cartoon dog on the plate with the red ketchup. At the last moment, he added a collar and dog tag. The finishing touch, one that appealed to him.

He turned the plate around and held it up for her, feeling absurdly like a child holding out a messy school project for a hard-to-please mother.

To his surprise, she laughed and clapped her hands. "Adorable," she said. "And the dog's not bad either."

Her approval fed something deep within him, something dormant and primal. "Thank you, ma'am."

How could he get that smile from her again? The smile that showed she was truly pleased, and not plotting how best to punish him?

Actually, the plotting-to-punish smile was pretty hot too.

She left fifteen minutes later after eating only half of her salad and accepting a refill on her soda, despite her subtle show of displeasure at being interrupted yet again.

Blake picked the bill off the table, not surprised to see the line on the bill that had a place for customers to add in a tip was crossed off.

What did surprise him was the business card tucked into the black plastic folder. He picked it up, fingering it gingerly.

*Victoria Sanders*, it read, followed by an email and cell number. Nothing else. Blake flipped it over in his hands, looking for more information about Victoria.

Fine handwriting filled the back of the card.

*You don't deserve a tip, little Blake,* it read.

*You deserve a spanking.*

*Call me if you agree.*

* * *

Blake took the subway home after work, Victoria's card tucked carefully into his wallet—next to his over-run credit card where he'd be sure not to lose it.

What was her note to him all about? Women pretty much never came on to him, at least not overtly. Had she even been coming on to him, or did she really just want to spank him? Or maybe the whole thing was a joke. A tease.

Maybe she never expected him to actually call her, to agree that he deserved a spanking more than a tip for his performance at the diner that afternoon.

Should he call?

*Fuck.*

Blake thought about it some more as he showered off the grime from the day. It was Friday night, which was usually when he went out bar-hopping with his roommates. They liked to get plastered on crazy-expensive Midtown beer and be each other's "wingman", whatever the hell that meant. Blake got lucky every so often, since he was surrounded by women at the community college where he was getting his associate's degree in business admin. But when he did get lucky, it wasn't with the type of woman he fantasized about. The type of older, dominating, hot, boot-wearing, take-no-shit woman—like Victoria.

His cock hardened once more, though this time he was free to do something about it with one soapy hand.

An image of Victoria forcing him to his knees in front of her made him quicken his strokes, gasping as the hot water slid over his face.

Okay. He'd call her. Fuck yeah, he'd call her.

\* \* \*

Victoria slipped out of her business suit, finally, after an overly-long drinks meeting with a literary agent. She still had a long night of reading ahead of her if she was going to find the right manuscript to fill the hole in her publishing imprint's schedule. Even after narrowing potential manuscripts through her editorial assistant, she still had to contend with the virtual slush pile filling her e-reader.

Standing in her bedroom, she relished the feel of air on her now naked skin. Her phone rang, her caller ID lighting up with an unknown number that appeared to have an out of state area code.

"Victoria speaking," she answered, all business. After all, even at ten o'clock on a Friday night, it could still be business. One of her authors in a crisis, perhaps.

"Um, Victoria? Ma'am?"

The boyish voice on the other end of the line triggered a smile. Ah yes. The waiter. The lovely little Blake.

"Who is this?" she asked. "And why are you calling me at this hour?"

"I'm so sorry, ma'am. You um...you gave me your card? I mean, this is Blake. From The '50's Diner. I was your waiter?"

As if she'd forget. His sweet pandering and the blush that heated his cheeks when she scolded him made her want to see how well his other cheeks heated up under her well-applied...scolding.

"Why are you calling me, Blake?" she asked, feigning ignorance of the message she'd written on the back of her card. In reality, she just wanted to hear him say it. To hear him admit how badly he deserved to be spanked over her knee.

His voice lowered. "Um, because of what you wrote on the back of your card."

"And what was that?"

"That I didn't deserve a tip," he said, obviously uncomfortable saying the words she wanted him to say. Good. It was more fun when she got to push a naughty young man out of his comfort zone.

"You're calling me at ten o'clock on Friday night," she said, enunciating each word, adding a tinge of incredulity, "because I didn't leave you a tip? Really?"

"No, ma'am," he hastened. Then, slowly, "You were right. I didn't deserve a tip."

"No? What do you deserve then?"

"Um..."

Victoria smiled in amusement at the phone, knowing he was unable to see her expression. "Tell me what you deserve or I'm hanging up."

"Um…"

"One. Two…" She moved the phone away from her ear, her finger poised above the End Call button.

"I…deserve a spanking," he whispered finally, his voice so low she barely heard it coming through the phone.

She put the receiver back to her ear. "What was that, little Blake? Speak up."

"I deserve a spanking." Louder this time, more resolutely.

"Listen carefully. It's 'I deserve a spanking *Ma'am*,'" she corrected, giving her title the proper tone of reverence she was due.

She could practically hear the desire in his voice, the raw need as he finally said the words she wanted to hear. "I deserve a spanking, Ma'am."

"Yes, little Blake, you do. And an extra punishment for disturbing my evening."

"I'm sorry, Ma'am."

"Not yet, you're not. But you will be. Tonight."

"Yes, Ma'am."

She gave him her address and hung up.

Victoria couldn't help but smile again. Blake was so eager, so young. He'd be a joy to train…and a pleasure to punish.

\* \* \*

Blake arrived at Victoria's apartment building and stood at the front door, uncertain how to proceed. A doorman held the door open for him and gestured him toward the elevator. Had she called down to let the doorman know to expect him?

He felt out of place here, like he'd stepped into a more successful world he wasn't supposed to be a part of for another few years. Perhaps another ten years. That had to be how much older Victoria was than him, perhaps more even.

She might be in her mid-thirties, although her glowing skin and flawless beauty didn't betray her age. Rather, her demeanor alone made her seem…authoritative.

Despite having relieved the tension he'd had in his cock since the moment he saw her at the diner earlier that day, Blake's desire only continued to grow unabated. Walking became torture as the turgid flesh beneath his boxer-briefs rubbed painfully against his zipper, the thin cotton doing little to ease the friction.

Apartment 4C. He raised his hand to knock when the door swung open.

Victoria stood in the doorway, wearing a tight pair of leather pants, four-inch stiletto- heeled black leather boots, and a lacy black tank-top that seemed at odds with her outfit, although it looked positively killer on her.

"Well?" she said, stepping aside. "Come in."

Blake smiled uncertainly and stepped inside, suddenly unsure why he'd come. Was he here to get laid? Because something told him she wouldn't just give it up that easily. So was it really about…getting spanked?

Why he would crave something he'd never actually experienced before, not even as a child, baffled him. He had no idea where the obsession came from.

*Well, maybe a few moments over Victoria's knee will drive that obsession right out of me—so I can grow up and start acting like a man, instead of like a boy who needs to be punished for being naughty.*

"This is the living room," Victoria said, interrupting his thoughts. "The bathroom is to the right. And the bedroom is down the hall. What is your last name, little Blake?"

"Claren, Ma'am," he answered dutifully. Even in her four-inch stiletto boots, Blake still had a couple inches on her. So why did she keep calling him 'little'?

Better question: why did he enjoy hearing her call him that, enjoy being spoken to like that?

"Then *Claren* is your safeword," she said. "That means if you want to stop whatever it is we're doing, then you say your safeword and you go home."

"What if I just want to use the safeword and all I need is a break, and then we could continue?" he asked, intrigued. He'd never been spanked before, what if he needed a breather? Although, from the looks of her, he couldn't imagine those tiny hands of her causing him anything other than pleasure.

"Needing a break is not a reason to use your safeword—I may be pushing you for a reason. Because it *hurts* is not a reason to use your safeword. You can guarantee if you play with me that I'm going to cause you plenty of pain."

Pain. Did he want pain? His cock throbbed in response. Okay, maybe he did. Or his cock did, and he was along for the ride.

"Do you understand?" she asked.

"Yes, Ma'am."

"Do you want to leave now?"

He didn't hesitate. "No, Ma'am."

"Then," she replied, her voice icy and firm. "Strip."

Blake fumbled with the buttons on his shirt, watching her as he finally disentangled himself from it. Waiting for her to strip too, but she didn't. She just looked at him with an expression somewhere between interest and amusement, as if he were a puppy in a cage at the mall, ready to be sold.

He stepped out of his pants, his aching cock grateful to not be rubbing against the metal zipper.

"Undies off too, little Blake."

He blushed and pushed his briefs down his thighs. Now he was completely naked and at her mercy, while she remained fully clothed as they stood several feet apart in her minimally decorated living room.

"Go fetch that welcome mat, the one just inside the door," she ordered.

He walked over to the mat and picked it up, uncomfortably aware of his naked ass facing her. The mat felt prickly and stiff in his hands as he brought it over to her. What on earth was this for?

"Drop it on the carpet," she said.

"Yes, Ma'am," he said, confused. He put the mat on the carpet in the middle of her living room.

"On your knees. On the mat."

He dropped to his knees, surprised by how quickly his skin howled in protest at the painfully prickly welcome mat, and looked up at her—once again struck by her beauty. What would happen to him now?

"You're lucky it's only your knees on my welcome mat," she said. "I could make you lay on it, cock-down. Every erection would only drive your cock harder into the spiky plastic mat. What do you think about that?"

Blake gulped. He thought it sounded terrible and terribly hot all at the same time. What the fuck was wrong with him?

Victoria sauntered forward, standing so close that the leather-clad juncture of her thighs pressed against his face. "Do you like my pussy?"

"Yes, Ma'am," he whispered, his voice muffled against her groin.

"Maybe if you're good I'll sit on your face and let you pleasure me until I decide I've had enough," she purred. "But once I have you on my bed, don't expect to be let go anytime soon."

"Yes, Ma'am." His cock bobbed ridiculously, as if it were nodding, agreeing with her terms. His knees ached in protest against the mat. He felt each individual plastic piece sticking into the tender skin.

"I like to be serviced for hours," she warned. "And if you stop, I'll turn around, keep my pussy right up against your mouth, and torture your cock and balls."

Blake gulped. Torture? He couldn't handle that. He was just here for—he gasped as she grabbed a fistful of his hair and lowered his face to the ground, right in front of the mat he kneeled on.

She looked down at him. "You may follow me to the bedroom on all fours. That's how I like my men—on their knees. Do you like that too?"

He followed at her heels down the hall, grateful to get off that "welcome" mat, even if the feel of hard plastic was replaced by the feel of equally hard wood under his hands and knees.

"Yes, Ma'am." *God, yes.*

"Faster, little Blake. I want you over my knee and ready for your spanking in the next ten seconds. And I'm counting."

\* \* \*

Victoria didn't look behind her to see if Blake was following her on his hands and knees, like a dog, to her bedroom for his spanking. Of course he was, why wouldn't he be?

Her bedroom had a queen-sized four-poster bed that had been a bitch to get into the apartment on moving day, but it had been worth the effort. It was nice to have convenient posts at each corner of the bed to tie her playmates to. Not that she'd trained a submissive in a while—there hadn't been anyone who'd caught her eye. She'd had to make do with visiting the clubs and flogging other Dommes' submissives, with their permission, naturally. The Domme's permission. Not the sub's. At least that was the pretense, anyway. In reality, Victoria understood that the sub's boundaries were discussed long before anyone else was invited to play.

"You're over your ten second mark, little Blake," she warned, though she hadn't been counting. She already knew it took longer than ten seconds to get from the living room to her bedroom on all fours. The task was designed so the young man would fail—the perfect excuse to increase the punishment as she saw fit.

She smiled down at him as she sat on her straight-backed, cushioned chair, situated next to the end of the bed. "Come here, you naughty boy, over my knee. You can rest your head on the edge of the bed and muffle your cries in my duvet."

Blake looked up at her from the floor with a conflicted look—a look she knew well. She'd seen it before. Shame at wanting to be hurt, desire, more shame, more lust, plus a touch of mischievousness as memories of his earlier misdeeds flitted through his mind.

He smiled at her uncertainly as if to remind himself it was just a game—and that she was just a girl—as he carefully draped his lean, muscled body over her lap, his cock pushing insistently against her leather-covered thigh, his torso supported by the bottom of the bed. His head turned to the side, one clean-shaven cheek resting on her plush, purple duvet cover.

"I'm going to wipe that smile off your face," she said, enjoying the look of surprise that crossed his face at her words. "The only one smiling here is going to be me, because I'm going to enjoy every second of this spanking, and you're going to wish you didn't deserve one so badly."

A small bottle of lavender-scented hand lotion sat tucked into the tote bag hanging on the side of her chair, and she reached over and pulled it out, squeezing a generous dollop onto her hands. His cock jerked against her lap, and she laughed.

"This isn't for that luscious cock of yours, you dirty boy." She rubbed the sweet-smelling lotion over her hands, and then onto his rounded buttocks. "I'm going to spank you so often, and so thoroughly, that I need to keep your skin supple, and smooth. I want you to feel every slap with as much sting as possible."

The perfectly presented bottom on her lap seemed to call out to her to be spanked, but she took her time, gently rubbing on the lotion as she spoke to him.

"You won't be able to sit comfortably for a week by the time I'm through with you. Every time you sit, you'll think of me, little Blake."

"Yes, Ma'am," he said. An undercurrent of desire filled his words.

"I'm going to warm you up with just a light start," she said, and raised her hand high, bringing it down on his ass cheek. "Lovely," she murmured as his skin became pink under her touch.

She spanked the other cheek now, making sure the two pink blotches matched before continuing equally, first one cheek and then the other. Just for fun, she spanked his sit spot, that one spot right on the crease between his thigh and his ass, where he'd have no choice but to sit tomorrow. No matter how he adjusted himself in his seat the following week, he'd be thinking of her. She'd make sure of it. This time, instead of alternating sides, she continued to spank just the one spot on one cheek, over and over. She wouldn't stop until she got some sort of noise out of him.

He was a stubborn boy, it seemed.

No matter. She enjoyed the feel of his ass heating up under her palm as she rained down the blows, one on top of the other, over and over. Finally, long after she'd have expected him to, he moaned, writhing as if to get out from under her hand. His cock ground against her, still fully erect.

Victoria laughed and counted five more spanks before switching to the other side and repeating the punishment there. It took him less time to moan this time, so she gave him an extra ten before stopping, just in case he was trying to pull one over on her.

Finally, she rested her palm on his heated buttocks, the warmth from her spanking rising up to her hand.

Blake stayed lying half on the bed, half over her lap. "I've never been spanked before," he said.

"And you haven't yet, either," she said. "I was just warming you up. Do you feel how warm your bottom is now? Now it's ready for the proper spanking you deserve, with my hairbrush."

She grinned as Blake turned his face down into the duvet, as if to muffle his cry of protest.

"I told you, little Blake, that you wouldn't sit comfortably for a week when I was done with you, and I always keep my promises. Did you think being so slow to get over my lap wouldn't get you more punishment? I gave you fair warning, I told you ten seconds, now didn't I?"

"Yes Ma'am," he said, his voice muffled by the duvet. She could tell he wanted her to start, perhaps so he could get it over with. These young college boys, they always thought they wanted a real Dominatrix to spank them, but once they were actually over her lap, they quickly realized the fantasy was more bearable—and much less painful—than the reality.

But his cock continued to grind against her.

"How hard do I have to spank you to make you go soft?" she wondered aloud. "Let's find out."

Her wooden hairbrush, with its merciless large round back, was always conveniently kept in her tote on her chair so it would be within reach—along with a few other items, such as the lotion. The nice thing about that lotion was it made even the lightest spanking that much more stinging.

She lifted the hairbrush and swung with her full strength onto his buttocks, feeling the muscle get pounded as she followed through with the stroke.

"Ma'am!" Blake howled, looking surprised by the new level of pain.

Since she'd done a thorough job of warming up his ass with the hand spanking, he'd be less likely to bruise from this—though she hadn't been making empty threats when she told him he wouldn't sit comfortably for a week.

"That's just one spank," she scolded. "What a crybaby you are. I'm adding an extra two for your insolence."

Blake nodded and buried his face in her duvet again, gripping the bedding as if to stop himself from climbing off her lap.

The second blow landed right on top of the last one, surprising the young man, no doubt, since he jumped.

"Keep moving, you'll only get more licks," she warned.

"I can't help it," he gasped. "Fuck, it hurts."

"Blake," she said calmly, "Do you know your safeword?"

He paused. "Yes Ma'am."

"Well?"

"I'm sorry, Ma'am. I deserve to be spanked, Ma'am." He pressed his face back into the duvet.

Victoria smiled, and took her sweet time finishing his spanking with the hairbrush, each blow harder than the last. He was being such a good boy, muffling his sobs in her duvet—she'd let him lick her pussy when she was done. She still hadn't decided whether she'd need to tie him to her bed first though, to make sure he wouldn't escape. He was so eager and willing she might be able to force him into remaining in place just with her orders alone.

She couldn't wait to sit on his face.

And something would have to be done about the sticky trail of pre-come he'd gotten all over her leather pants during his spanking…

\* \* \*

Blake winced, biting his lip and gripping the duvet tightly to avoid letting another sound escape his lips. He'd dreamed—no, *obsessed*—about being spanked by a hot Domme his entire adult life—but now that he was actually here he wished he could be anywhere else. He knew it would hurt, wanted it to hurt, even. But he'd had no idea it would hurt as much as it did.

She was still going, slamming her wicked hairbrush against his ass, forever changing the way he would think about the concept of 'a spanking.'

*Fuck.*

He'd slipped into a place where he stopped thinking entirely, his entire being focused solely on his burning ass cheeks and the sound of the hairbrush whipping through the air, the *thwack* as it connected with his skin.

Her voice cut through his fog. "Have you had enough, little Blake?"

"Yes, Ma'am," he said.

The hairbrush lay on his lower back as if she considered his words. "No, I don't believe you have."

She finally stopped after another few strokes, but he didn't dare move, certain she was just gearing up to start again.

"You took your medicine so well," she purred, rubbing more of that sweet-smelling lotion on his skin.

Something hard pressed against his mouth and he opened his eyes warily. The evil wooden hairbrush.

"Kiss the brush and thank me for disciplining you," she ordered.

He didn't hesitate. The wood seemed to be a warm, alive thing under his lips. "Thank you, Ma'am."

"Get down, on your knees in front of me."

Unwilling to risk having her change her mind, he hurried to obey. There were so many things he could do on his knees in front of her—such as worship her with his head securely tucked between her slender thighs.

This was everything he'd ever dreamed of. To be on his knees in front of a beautiful woman who'd just spanked the hell out of him. *Yesssss.*

"Look what you've done to my nice leather pants," Victoria said.

*Oh shit.*

Her lap was covered in a slick trail of his own pre-come.

"I'm sorry, Ma'am."

"I *was* going to let you show your gratitude properly," she breathed, pulling his head to her groin as if to show him exactly what she meant. "But then I see you've already had plenty of fun, and without my permission."

He hung his head, willing his cock to go down, but he was aroused to the point of no return. He had to do whatever it took to please her so she'd invite him back for another spanking.

"You'll have to clean my pants, of course," she said.

"Of course, Ma'am. I'll pay for your dry-cleaning." Having such nice leather pants cleaned was going to seriously cut into his already minimal budget, since all his money from being a waiter went toward buying textbooks and rent.

Her laughter surprised him, and he looked up at her face. "Not quite. You will clean my pants with your tongue."

Blake looked at the shiny wet trails of his own pre-come on her pants with trepidation. Lick up his own pre-come? The thought of being forced to submit to Victoria in such a way turned him on even as it made his stomach do flip-flops.

"When you're done, I'll let you put your tongue to use in a way you may find more enjoyable," she murmured.

*Fuck.*

He needed to see that pussy, to savor her scent and her taste. To bury himself between her legs for hours.

Which meant he needed to get to work so he could get his reward.

He took a deep breath and leaned forward, sticking his tongue out gingerly, and licked at one sticky line on her tight leather pants.

"Hurry up, now," she said. "We don't have all day for you to savor your own juice."

He went for it, the salty taste and slippery texture assaulting his tongue as he licked her pants clean. She squirmed under his quick tongue.

Holy shit, she was getting off on just feeling his mouth through her leather! Knowing that made the task fucking hotter than he'd ever have imagined licking up his own come would be.

When he was done, he leaned back on his heels with a satisfied smile.

"You just love to lick up come, don't you?" she said.

*What?* "No, Ma'am. I mean, yes. I love to do whatever you tell me to do, I think."

"I see," she laughed. "Is that why that gorgeous cock of yours is trying to salute me?"

He grinned at her words. It was nice to hear she liked his cock, even if it was unnerving how easily she gave him erections just by ordering him around.

"Lie down on the bed," she said, her tone different now, softer. "Face up."

Her soft duvet beckoned him, but he covered his cock with one hand to keep from leaving another embarrassing trail of his arousal on the cover as he lay down.

"Lace your hands behind your head."

Victoria pulled her boots off—at least he imagined she did from the sound of them hitting the floor. He couldn't see more than the ceiling and whatever was in his peripheral vision unless he lifted his head, which seemed like cheating, somehow, since she hadn't told him he could do it. She stood at the foot of the bed and pulled off her leather pants.

"So nice," she sighed, "to feel air on my skin again."

He had to see. Lifting his head, he got one quick glance of her naked legs and waxed pussy before she laughed, and he dropped his head back onto his laced hands quickly.

"Are you ready, little Blake?" She crept onto the bed beside him and kneeled above him, one knee firmly planted on either side of his face. Her pussy glistened in front of him like a piece of freshly cut fruit, ready to be eaten.

* * *

Victoria brought her pussy down onto Blake's face, wanting him to feel the weight of her, to feel enveloped by her wetness, suffocated by it.

"Lick," she ordered, and gasped as he complied. He sucked her clit full into his mouth, rolling it between his lips and tongue.

When she'd spanked him and made him lick her through her leather pants she'd been so hot for him, even though she didn't want to show it. To have him on his knees and doing something that required quite a bit of submission had aroused her to the point where she could have come with just the slightest touch to her clit.

"Faster," she breathed.

He licked her pussy, moving his mouth and jaw so rapidly there was no way he could keep up the pace.

Good. Let that strong jaw of his get tired—she'd still be here, sitting on his face for as long as she desired.

That thought, along with Blake's talented tongue, brought on a crashing orgasm. She controlled herself, not wanting to break the kid's nose with her bucking hips, but she didn't hold back her moans of pleasure as she climaxed.

She lifted her hips, her knees still planted on either side of his handsome face. Her juices covered his lips as he grinned up at her.

"Not tired yet?" she asked, smiling back.

"Nope. I mean, no Ma'am."

"Lick me again," she said, but this time, she didn't move to sit on his face.

"Ma'am?" he asked, obviously confused.

"Sit up and do it."

He moved his hands from behind his head and used them to hold himself up on his elbows so he had better access to her pussy.

"I didn't say you could move your hands, now did I? Lie back down."

Blake fell back and laced his hands behind his head. "Sorry, Ma'am."

"Try again. I said I want you to lick my pussy. Sit up and keep your hands where they are."

Blake grunted as he basically did a half-sit up, holding himself up with his abdominal muscles, his hands still laced behind his head. God he looked good, his muscles straining, his abs looking like the perfect six-pack. No, eight-pack.

"Lick."

Victoria kept a stern expression on her face, but she couldn't help but feel aroused by the sudden realization dawning on Blake's face. She was going to make him eat her pussy in a very awkward position, one he couldn't possibly stay in comfortably.

And if he had to lie back a bit to ease his burning muscles, then she had the perfect excuse to punish him some more. Win-win.

Blake's tongue slipped out past his lips, millimeters away from her pussy as she maintained her position on her knees above his face. He forced himself up a bit more and finally reached her wet slit.

Knowing he was probably already experiencing some muscle pain from the impromptu workout made his mouth feel all the sweeter when he finally brought his lips and tongue onto to her, licking her with renewed vigor.

He groaned against her pussy but continued to lick her, a sheen of sweat breaking out on his forehead.

"Tired yet?" she asked, playfully moving away another inch so he had to pull his abs even tighter to reach her.

"Yes Ma'am," he grunted.

"I thought you wanted to lick my pussy?"

"Please, Ma'am," he said, falling back onto her pillow, heaving a sigh as his muscles finally relaxed after being in a contracted sit-up position for so long.

"I see, you don't like pussy," she teased. "I should have guessed as much when I saw how much you loved to lick up your own come."

"I love pussy," he said. "I mean, I love *your* pussy, Ma'am."

"And yet here I offer my pussy—my shrine—to you, and you lay back down and refuse to lick it because of a little discomfort?"

While she wasn't really upset with him, the look of confusion and concern that crossed his face at her words thrilled her. She loved messing with her subs' heads, twisting their words and making them unsure of themselves. It was one more way she was able to enjoy her dominance over them.

And Blake, being so completely new to the game, was even more fun to play with because he didn't seem to know that she was only teasing him—that there was no way he'd ever win with her, no way he'd ever not be punished for an infraction, no matter how hard he tried to be good.

If he was always good, it ruined the fun, now didn't it?

"No, I don't think you like pussy," she continued. "I think you like ass."

He raised his eyebrows at her words, which made her smile.

"Since you're lying back so comfortably, I'm going to let you stay there while I turn around. What do you think of that?"

"I'll pleasure you however you want me to, Ma'am—I've just never done that before. Ever."

"Then now's a good time to practice," she said, turning around so she straddled him backwards, looking at his feet, which seemed to tremble with the effort of keeping still. "Soon you'll be begging for my ass on your lips."

"Ma'am," he said, and she could feel him shaking his head *No* against the back of her thighs, his hair tickling her skin. But even still, soon he began licking the sensitive nerve endings surrounding her rosebud.

She'd showered immediately before he came over, so she knew she was clean, but the very dirty taboo of sitting backwards on her waiter's face and making him lick her asshole made her moan with pleasure.

His cock stood at attention in front of her, the tip glistening with pre-come. She reached out and carefully touched his slit with one long fingernail. He moaned in response, his breath hot on her ass, and lifted his hips up as if begging for more contact.

"You want more, little Blake?" she asked, circling his cock with the long fingernails on her left hand. She kept the right-hand nails short, perfect for penetrating a tight ass to ease its way up to being fucked by her strap-on, something she loved to do.

But little Blake didn't know that about her yet.

\* \* \*

Blake gingerly licked at Victoria's asshole. It wasn't bad, not like he imagined it would be. Not that he'd ever imagined eating someone's ass. She tasted clean, though, like her pussy had, and her skin had the faint scent of the sweet-smelling lavender lotion she'd rubbed on his butt before she wailed on it.

Even now while lying on the bed he kept wanting to shift positions to keep the weight off his bruised bottom. She hadn't been kidding when she said he wouldn't sit comfortably any time soon. Damn, she knew what she was talking about.

If only she'd grab his cock, or at least let him take matters into his own hands. He'd built up enough come to last him a decade. If he didn't shoot soon, he'd die of blue balls, and fuck anyone who said you can't die from blue balls.

He wiggled his tongue around her asshole, eliciting the sexiest moan he'd ever heard. There was something about Victoria that made him want to do whatever she desired. Eating ass may not be his thing, but being told to eat her ass and submitting to her will definitely was.

No wonder his cock was so hard it hurt.

She ran her fingernail lightly down his shaft, and he groaned from the pleasure-pain of it. "Please," he said. "I want to be inside of you. Please, Victoria. Ma'am."

She stilled, and his breath caught in his throat. Had he gone too far? Had he said the wrong thing?

Victoria turned around and sat on the bedside next to him, where he still lay with his hands laced behind his head, his legs outstretched.

"So," she said, trailing her fingernail around his nipple. "You want to have sexual intercourse."

The emphasis she put on the words *sexual intercourse* threw him. Was it so strange that after licking her most intimate places, after all they'd just done together, that he'd want to have sex? As much as he loved everything that had happened so far that evening, at some point he wanted to be able to slip inside her wet heat and hold her in his arms as he fucked her until they were both screaming in ecstasy.

Somehow he had a feeling that wouldn't happen with Victoria. She didn't seem like the type of woman who'd be willing to get fucked. But maybe she could fuck him. He'd lie back and let her do all the work if that's what she really wanted.

What was the right thing to say? She kept twisting his words, so speaking around her had become an impossible way to communicate, it seemed.

He opted for the truth. "I really like you, Ma'am."

She laughed, smiling down at him from her seat at his side on the bed. "How sweet."

*Do you like me?* He didn't dare ask, not if he wanted to preserve some semblance of dignity. It was doubtful she actually liked him, or thought of him as more than her naughty and incompetent waiter.

*Then why did she invite me over?*

"I think, little Blake, that you just want to come, and you're saying whatever you can think of to get what you want."

"Ma'am," he started, unsure of himself yet again. "Of course I want to come. But I also really do like you. And…um, I'd like to see you again."

He thought he caught a fleeting smile on her beautiful face, but it was gone so quickly he may have imagined it.

"Don't move," she ordered, and she reached over him, rustling around in her bedside table drawer.

Blake lay as still as he could, certain that if she even caught him breathing too fast she'd call the whole thing off. What was she going to do?

"You want to have sex, Blake?" She pulled herself away from him and sat up so he could see what she held in her hand. In one hand, a condom and a little bottle of lube.

In the other, a thin dildo with a flared base.

*Oh, fuck.*

"Answer me," she said. "Do you want to fuck me?" She set down the dildo and tore open the condom wrapper, sheathing his cock in one smooth motion.

"Yes," he breathed, so ready to come he gasped at the feel of her hand stroking his length when she put the condom on him. "Please, Ma'am," he added for good measure.

"Well then. We must play fair. For every thrust you give me, I get to return it in kind. Agreed?"

Blake hoped she meant that she'd roll her luscious hips onto him, moving herself on his cock, but he knew from the way her devious mind seemed to work that the long, thin dildo had something to do with her idea of "fair play."

He groaned. Nothing had ever gone up his ass before, and he never intended anything to go up there. It was exit only as far as he was concerned. But he needed to come so badly, needed to be inside of her.

"I'm going to fuck your ass with my dildo while we have sex," she said, in no uncertain terms. "That is the only way I will have sex with you tonight. You do remember your safeword, now don't you?"

Blake nodded. Should he call her out? Go home and jack off? No, because jacking off would never be as good as actually being inside of Victoria. If he left now, there was no way she'd ever see him again.

And he had to see her again.

"Then we're agreed," she said. Then, to his surprise, she leaned over and brushed her lips over his ear in an almost-kiss. "Don't worry, I'll be gentle."

Suddenly he felt scared, the way he imagined that shy virgin he'd slept with from his Lit 101 class might have felt right before her cherry popped.

"Bend your knees up," she said, and he did, still lying on his back. His bruised butt cheeks welcomed the change in position, but he knew he was about to experience a new kind of erotic pain. His asshole tightened in anticipation.

*Oh, fuck.*

* * *

Victoria straddled him backwards, facing his bent legs, and admired his knees. They were beautiful knees, not knobby at all. Faint scars marred his skin, as if Blake had been an exceptionally accident-prone child.

His hard cock stood upright in front of her pussy, just waiting for her to mount it. She'd been looking forward to riding this young man since the moment he stuttered out his apologies at the diner earlier that day. Now was her chance.

Rising up, she brought herself down on his cock, millimeter by millimeter, her thigh muscles quivering with her effort to drag out the sensation of first penetration. Finally, she sank down to his balls with a moan of pleasure.

Too bad she couldn't see his face to gauge his expression, since she was facing his ass. With his knees up, she could see his still-reddened ass cheeks, just waiting to be spread and invaded by her dildo.

Blake lifted his hips up, grinding his cock inside of her. With a quick slap downward between his bent legs, she spanked his ass. "No moving, young man. This is my ride, and I'm in charge."

"Yes, Ma'am."

She leaned forward to reach down and spread his ass cheeks, revealing the taut hole, surrounded by dark crinkly pubic hair that matched the thatch above his cock. *Oh my, that's a nice ass.* And leaning forward had the fortuitous side-effect of pressing the head of his cock directly against her G-spot.

For her own pleasure, she circled her hips, reveling in the stimulation inside her. From the sounds Blake made behind her, however, he was enjoying himself way too much.

Time to change that.

She picked up the dildo and sheathed it in a condom, rubbing lube up and down the length. Leaning forward once more, she pressed the slender tip against Blake's virgin asshole.

"Oh God, no," Blake murmured, as she inserted the dildo just one inch.

She stopped, pausing with the dildo part-way inside of him, her pussy still impaled on his cock. "Blake," she said sharply. "Do you know your safeword?"

"Yes, Ma'am."

"Well?"

He groaned as she slid up and down his cock once more, letting him feel her pussy clamp down on him. "I'm not using my safeword, Ma'am. I want you to fuck me."

"Then tell me you want me to fuck your ass, Blake. I want to hear you say it."

This time, she could hear the tremor in his voice. Poor dear, she'd have to train him to not be so hesitant in response to her plans for him. The dildo she was using on him was nothing, slimmer than the average cock, even. Nothing compared to the monster strap-on she liked to use on her subs once they were sufficiently anally-trained.

Too bad Blake was nowhere near ready for that. In the future, perhaps.

Definitely in the future.

"I want," he took a breath. "Um, I want you to fuck my ass, Ma'am."

"It would be my pleasure," she said graciously, and thrust the dildo deep inside him up to the flared base, delighting in the wail she elicited.

"Stroke for stroke," she reminded him, and slid up and down his cock slowly once before pulling the dildo out of his ass almost all the way. Watching his tight anus stretch open as she maneuvered the toy was enough to bring her to the edge of climax.

Still, she'd promised him stroke for stroke, and that is what she'd deliver. Circling her hips, she rode him up and down again. His breath hitched in anticipation when she reached down between his bent legs and thrust the dildo in and out of his ass.

"Oh fuck, oh fuck," he said, and from the rustling behind her, she knew he was thrashing his head back and forth against her pillow.

She knew she was fucking his cock with her pussy way too slowly for him to come. It was the equivalent of her running her hand up and down his cock once every few seconds at a glacial speed. Sure, it may have felt nice, but it was its own form of cock torture to deny a man his orgasm, to draw it out as long as possible.

Clenching her inner muscles around his length, she slowly moved up and down once more.

Blake moaned.

"Do you like it when I use your cock for my pleasure, and my pleasure alone?" she asked, delighting in the idea of making him think she wouldn't let him come.

Suddenly, Blake's hands were on her hips, the large fingers digging into her flesh. He'd moved from position— something she'd train right out of him soon enough. Those hands were supposed to be laced behind his head until she gave him permission to move.

He'd just earned himself a major punishment, and he didn't even know it yet.

\* \* \*

Blake groaned, grasping Victoria's hips as she sat facing away from him, torturing him with her slow ride and the dildo she'd been carefully fucking his ass with. His asshole burned as if she'd been licking it with a flame.

She turned her head, looking back over her shoulder at him, her dark hair slipping into her face like a veil. "Just what do you think you're doing?"

"Victoria," he said, thrusting his hips up, forcing himself deeper inside her wet cunt, "I need more."

With that, he slammed into her, hard and fast, fucking her as best he could while he was still flat on his back. It felt so good to finally scratch that itch—to have all that friction flowing over his cock.

*She's going to kill me for this.* He knew he wasn't being a very good submissive if he was trying to show her who's boss by fucking the shit out of her.

But to his surprise, Victoria just threw her head back and gasped, her face contorted on the edge of orgasm. She took a deep breath, as if to pull herself together.

"You want to play rough?" she asked, leaning forward between his knees and thrusting the dildo into his ass again. "Stroke for stroke, darling." With that, she ceased the careful initiation into anal play and slammed the dildo in hard right up to the base. Before he could catch his breath, she pulled it out, his ass screaming from the erotic pain of it all, and slammed it in again.

"You want to fuck me, Blake? Then you better be able to take it as well as you can give it."

Blake didn't hold back a howl of pain as she fucked his ass fast and rough, just like he'd been fucking her pussy only a moment ago.

Defeated, he let go of her hips and stopped trying to run the show. Now that she was no longer held in place by his grip she lifted herself off his cock and settled down next to him.

"I'm not done yet, little Blake—you still need to be shown who does the fucking in this bedroom." She poked at his ass again with the dildo, this time twisting it mercilessly.

"You win," he gasped, forcing himself to breathe through the onslaught.

She laughed and pulled the dildo out of him. He could have sworn his asshole slammed shut like a frightened little clam once she had the damn thing out of him.

"You're so cute," she said, yanking the condom off his erection. "Fucking me like a man, when just moments ago you were over my knee like a naughty boy."

She flicked her fingers against his cock, once, twice, and then…he came. Spurted his come all over his abs and thighs; so much came out because he'd been holding it in since he first arrived at her apartment.

Fuck. How did she do that to him?

Victoria sighed and lay back onto the bed next to him, her face mere inches from his. "What a good boy you are," she murmured. "I liked that. Did you?"

He took quick inventory of himself—asshole on fire, butt-cheeks tender, muscles aching, cock wilted and spent. "Yeah," he grinned. "I liked it a lot."

She ran her finger over one of his flat nipples. "I think you mean, 'yes, Ma'am.'"

"Yes, Ma'am."

God, she was gorgeous. "You know what I just realized?" Blake asked, looking into her deep brown eyes.

"What?" The hard edge gone from her voice, she was all satin and sweetness now, sleepy almost.

"I've just had the most incredible sex of my life, and we've never even kissed."

Victoria propped herself up on one elbow, returning his gaze. "A kiss from me is special. I don't kiss my subs, usually. It's a privilege I allow…infrequently."

"I see." Blake didn't like the idea of her having other subs—other men who came into her bedroom. He wanted to be the only one, which was crazy—they'd only just met. What was it about her that made him feel that way?

She checked the time on the cell phone sitting on her bedside table. "You'll have to go now," she said, "it's getting late and I have a lot of manuscripts to read for work."

Blake took the hint. Not even a subtle hint. She didn't want to kiss him, she had plenty of other dudes on the side, and she needed him to get out of her apartment.

*Fuck.*

He went into her bathroom and dressed quickly, wiping his come off his body with a wet towel. At the front door, he shivered as he stepped on her welcome mat, remembering the pain it had given his knees for even the few moments she made him kneel on it.

She must have noticed him looking at the mat, because she said "When a man is particularly naughty I make him sit on that mat after a spanking. Really drives the point home, so to speak."

The thought of sitting on the prickly plastic mat, even without a bruised butt, was enough to send goosebumps up and down his arms. So why did it turn him on?

He cleared his throat. "I deserve a punishment like that, Ma'am. Whatever you want me to do, I'm—I'm…at your service. Whenever you want me."

Blake held his breath, hoping she wouldn't reject him too harshly, although after the stunt he pulled in the bedroom, holding her hips in place while he slammed his cock into her, he wouldn't be surprised if she slammed the door in his face.

Instead, Victoria smiled. "You want to come back for more punishment, huh?"

God yes. He had no idea why, but yes, yes, yes. Before he could respond, Victoria placed her hand on his cheek and drew him into her, his mouth so very close to her luscious lips. He didn't dare kiss her, not after she told him that it was a privilege she allowed infrequently.

But then—she kissed him, pressing her lips to his, her tongue gently parting his lips and dancing in his mouth. When she pulled back, she was smiling again.

It was the smile she'd given him at the diner after he'd drawn her a dog out of ketchup. The smile that said she was happy and that she approved. That she was pleased with him.

This was the smile he'd been looking for since he first arrived at her apartment.

"I'll be seeing you," she said, and shut the door.

*The End*

# DENIED BY HER: NOVELLA 2

Blake Claren felt that familiar sense of adrenaline mixed with lust pooling in his gut as he rode the elevator up to Victoria's apartment. They'd been dating for the past month, if dating was the right word for what they were doing. Which it wasn't. How could they be dating if he'd never been on an actual date with her? No, their encounters always happened late at night, in the warm darkness of her luxurious Midtown apartment.

He'd only seen her during the day once, when she was still a stranger to him instead of the intimate lover she'd become. That was the day he waited on her at the '50s-themed diner where he worked to pay for his textbooks, and instead of a tip she left him her number along with an admonition that he needed to be spanked.

*Fuck, had that really been only a month ago?* It felt like he'd known her forever, although maybe that was just because she seemed to instinctively understand his more primal desires. The desire to serve her, to take care of her, to be dominated by her, and to be used by her as she wished.

And man she was really good at that. But tonight he had a reason to be nervous, and not just because he never knew what sort of wicked punishment Victoria would come up with for him when he entered her home. Tonight, he'd have to confess that he'd failed his English Lit midterm.

It was the sort of thing she loved to ask him about when he was over her knee.

*How are you doing in school, little Blake? Are you studying hard so you can be as successful as I know you're capable of being?*

And he'd promise her up and down that he was being a good student and studying hard. Fuck. The faceless door to apartment 4C loomed before him, and he hesitated, his finger a millimeter away from the doorbell.

*Ring it, damn it. Confess and take your punishment. You know you want to.*

He did want to, even as his finger trembled at the thought. What would she do to him when she found out he'd actually failed a test? What if she decided to stop seeing him so he'd have more time to study?

The door opened before he had a chance to ring it.

"Are you trying to keep me waiting, young man?" Victoria asked with a smile on her red lips. Her tight leather skirt accentuated her slender legs in black fishnet stockings. He hoped they were the crotchless ones she'd worn once before.

"No, Ma'am, I wasn't trying to keep you waiting."

"Then I think you're standing there, trying to figure out how to hide something from me." She turned and walked back into her living room and he followed.

*How does she know me so well?*

Victoria sat back on her couch and lifted a glass of red wine to her lips, but she only took the tiniest of sips. "Strip."

"Yes, Ma'am." He was grateful for an order, something to do that would take his mind off his failing grade. Why couldn't he do well at school, the way he wanted to? It didn't take him long to strip off the T-shirt and jeans he'd worn to her house. He never bothered to dress to impress, knowing Victoria preferred him to be completely naked around her and at her mercy. And if he was honest with himself, and honesty was something she insisted on, he liked it too.

"Come here," she ordered, pointing to the floor in front of her. "I need a footrest."

Blake felt heat rise to his cheeks at the new request, but he hurried to obey. He would happily be furniture for her, if that's what pleased her. Kneeling on all fours in front of her, he strived to flatten his posture into what he hoped would be a suitable footrest. Her stiletto boots scraped slowly across the skin on his back before coming to a stop.

The weight of her feet and boots on his naked back made his cock spring to life. It surprised him on a regular basis how the most simple request from her had the ability to make him so hard.

"I like this footrest," she murmured. Blake couldn't see her from his position, but he imagined she'd taken another sip of her wine. "Turn around, footrest. Face away from me."

He moved on all fours, her feet still resting on his back. His ass was now right in front of her. Fuck. It was a very vulnerable position to be in, especially near Victoria, who seemed to have a penchant for torturing his ass with spankings hard enough to make a grown man cry and with dildos to make his asshole hers for the taking.

Her black stiletto boot slid off his back, scraping his skin as she pressed her boot to his ass, then she dropped the toe of her boot down, nudging his hanging testicles.

*Oh God no.*

She tapped his balls carefully with her boot, sending a flow of erotic pain mixed with nausea through him. This was never in his fantasy playbook, never something he'd have thought he wanted. But knowing he was presenting his undefended balls to her boot to do what she wanted with them made his cock stay hard, a drop of pre-come beading on the tip.

"Put your head and shoulders down on the floor," she said, and he obeyed immediately, despite the fear her words inspired.

"Good boy," she said, moving her boot back to his ass. "Now reach back and spread your cheeks for me. I want to see your sweet little asshole."

Blake moaned but reached back and spread his ass for her, his position so uncomfortable he wasn't sure how long he could hold it.

Victoria laughed behind him. "Have you ever heard the saying, 'I'm going to kick your ass?'"

"Yes, Ma'am," he replied, barely able to speak through his fast breathing.

"Most people who say they're going to kick someone's ass don't actually do that, now do they, little Blake?"

"No, Ma'am." He struggled to maintain his position, his face and shoulders pressed against her plush carpet, his ass in the air, and his arms reaching back to spread his ass cheeks open to reveal his most intimate area. The fact that she wasn't doing anything to him scared the hell out of him. When would it happen? *What* would happen?

* * *

Victoria took another sip of her Merlot and sighed contentedly. This was the life. She'd had a lovely day at work—finally snagging an author she'd been hoping to work with for the new line her publisher had entrusted her with—and it was nice to come home to a strapping young man ready to take the abuse she loved to dole out.

Perfection.

His asshole seemed to wink at her, to look at her tensely in anticipation. Well, she wouldn't keep his frightened little bottom waiting any longer.

"Do you know how beautiful you look to me, little Blake, in this position? I think you get off on knowing that a woman is about to kick your ass. Tell me I'm right."

She loved messing with his head, and could barely contain her delight. If he said she was right, that he was turned on, then he had to admit to himself his deep, base desire to submit. It was something she was working on with him. But if he said no, then she got to punish him until he said yes. Win-win.

"You're right, Ma'am," he replied earnestly, his words slightly muffled by his face in the carpet. "I get off on doing whatever you want."

Unexpected, but a lovely answer. She'd been training him well. Still had to punish him, of course.

"What I want is for you to be a footrest. Hold still," she ordered. "Footrests don't move."

Slowly, carefully, she flexed her foot in her boot and inserted the heel of her stiletto into his tight little asshole. The heel was so thin that it went in smoothly, even without lube.

Blake moaned, a sound that made her wet every time. She loved to hear the sounds he made when she played with him. He was so dramatic and vocal, even when he thought he was being stoic. Silly boy. She pumped her boot in him a couple of times just to hear him moan again.

With a quick move, she pulled her heel back and out of his ass and pushed the toe of her boot right onto his tender hole, pushing him forward onto his stomach.

"Look at that," she mused, satisfied with his responsiveness to her. "Girls really do kick ass. Now stand up."

Victoria set her barely-touched wine glass aside and watched with interest as he stood and faced her. His erection stood at attention, so hard it looked painful, the veins bulging along the sides of his thick shaft.

"You must love it when I violate your ass," she remarked, rising from the couch to stand in front of him.

A look of lust crossed his handsome face, and he hung his head as if to shield her from his desire. His dark, shaggy hair fell into his eyes, and he looked so adorable it took no small amount of willpower to not brush the hair out of them.

"Well? I can't hear you," she said.

She hid her smile when he couldn't answer, couldn't admit that he loved it when she fucked him with her stiletto boot, loved it when she made him her footrest.

"You have an appointment with my paddle," she said, and walked down the hall to her bedroom. She didn't need to glance back to know that Blake was following her like an eager puppy. His whole-hearted devotion to her games made him even more appealing to her.

This time, she had a surprise for him. She knew he'd be getting his grade back for his midterm this week at college, and no matter what grade he got, he'd have to be punished for it. He'd been studying, she supposed, but he never spoke much about it with her. Anything less than an A+ could easily justify the scene she'd cooked up for him.

Blake entered her bedroom and stood in the doorway. His mouth literally dropped open like a gaping fish at the sight. She laughed. How could she not? That face!

The big black school chalkboard had been easy to find, and her experience with hanging paintings had proven helpful in securing it to the wall facing her bed, so she could lie back and watch him write lines if she wished. The old-style wooden school desk with the attached chair had been harder to find, but she'd done it thanks to eBay. She'd been debating getting the desk ever since she first met Blake and discovered he was actually a real live naughty schoolboy. He wouldn't even have to pretend. Yes, he was twenty-three, but he went to college, and that meshed with so many of her fantasies. She could be his strict school teacher—a role she'd been born to play. If she hadn't gotten a job in publishing, she could easily see herself as a college professor teaching English.

Victoria's favorite piece in her new bedroom décor, however, was the simple wooden stool in the corner of her bedroom, ready for a freshly-paddled submissive to sit and think about his behavior. It was just so…old school, corner time. And she happened to know it was one of Blake's secret fantasies as well—one they hadn't had a chance to explore together before.

"Do you have something you want to confess? I think you're hiding something from me, little Blake."

Blake was still looking around the room in shock.

"Bend over the desk," she said, and watched with amusement as he slowly bent his lean frame over the wooden desktop, his cock pressing against the metal side.

Usually she enjoyed having him lie over her knee, where she could rub lotion onto his bottom and alternately spank and scold him, but tonight was different. Tonight, he was her schoolboy. She knew he had a big midterm grade to tell her about—she just didn't know what it was.

"Five licks for not telling me your grade immediately," she said, and brandished a paddle she'd owned for so long she'd almost forgotten she had it. Despite having Blake at her disposal— a sub with the sort of apple-ass that cried out to be paddled— she'd yet to use it on him.

\* \* \*

Blake eyed the large, scary-looking paddle she lowered to his eye-level as he lay across the wood desk. The surface of the desk felt cool and worn beneath his naked torso, but it was probably one of the most uncomfortable things she could have dreamed up for him to be spanked on. With his cock pressed against the cold metal side of the desk, his butt stuck out and his abs touched the top of the desk. His arms draped over the attached chair, but the top edge of the chair dug into his arms, and he couldn't figure out a better way to stabilize himself.

"I don't believe you've met Mr. Paddle, now have you?" Victoria's voice said from behind him as she brought the paddle out of his eye-line. It was behind him now. Fuck.

"Usually," she purred, rubbing his ass cheeks with her cold hand, "I like to give a light hand-spanking before I subject a boy to Mr. Paddle, so he won't get bruised. I like to warm them up."

He tensed even as desire coursed through him at her words. A hand spanking from Victoria was no laughing matter. She spanked hard. Really hard.

"But tonight I think you need to get your assed bruised so you remember your lesson. What do you think, little Blake? Do you deserve a bruised ass?"

"Yes, Ma'am. I know I do." A month ago, before he met her, those words would need to be cajoled out of him. But any idea that a grown man getting spanked by a woman half his size might be weird had been…well, spanked out of his very mindset. Knowing that he deserved—and wanted—whatever his Domme dished out had become part of his every day, walking–around thought process.

*I wonder how that happened so fucking fas—*

The first blow from the paddle came hard and fast, before he even had time to prepare himself. A shocked wail escaped his lips, and he bit back the noise with embarrassment.

Victoria slammed the paddle against his ass again. "I want you to remember this paddling, young man. Every time you sit down to study and it hurts, you'll remember why you better study hard."

"Yes, Ma'am," he gasped, as she paddled him again.

"You're getting two more, but I think you deserve much, much more, don't you?"

His ass hurt so badly already. The muscles were pounded, the skin burned. But he did deserve much more, and he knew the reason why.

She spanked him again in his silence, and he sobbed tearlessly, grateful for the release. But he wouldn't feel completely absolved until he told her the truth. As if sensing he might be ready to confess, Victoria paused, resting the wooden paddle on his ass as she spoke.

"I know you got your grades back this week, but you never told me how it went. So tell me now. What grade did you get on your midterm?"

Blake couldn't answer. God, she was a fucking editor, for Christ's sake. English Literature was her thing. And he'd gotten a failing grade in English Lit. How could he tell her that? What if his failure proved to her they could never be a real couple?

*Why should that matter?*

But it did. After a month of dating, or meeting up for sex—whatever this thing they had going was—it mattered. Because…he liked her a lot.

*Smack!* The shock of the paddle's impact forced the confession from him immediately.

"I failed my midterm, Ma'am." God, he'd be shit out of luck if he ever had the misfortune to be interrogated. They wouldn't even have to stick a single needle under his nail, he'd squeal like a pig as soon as they sat him down.

That was what this spanking reminded him of.

So why was he still hard as a fucking rock?

The paddle picked up a rhythm, punctuating Victoria's words with smacks. "You failed?" *Smack*. "Actually and truly failed?" *Smack*. "You've screwed up." *Smack*. "Big time." *Smack*. "You'll be punished for this."

*Wait—this wasn't the punishment?* He could barely think about anything but the sensations she inflicted on his bruised ass. Probably a good thing, because otherwise he'd start thinking of all the ways she could still punish him.

44

Finally, after what seemed like an eternity, she stopped. "On your knees, young man."

Blake struggled to get off the desk without rubbing his butt—so not worth the extra five spanks that move would earn him—and dropped to his knees in front of her, looking up at her the way he knew she liked, to show her that she had his complete attention. In his fantasies, before he met Victoria, he always imagined he'd have to look at the floor or something, but Victoria was a bit different that way.

She was the only real Domme he'd ever met, so he couldn't be sure.

"I'm disappointed in you, Blake," she said. Her voice was so serious, devoid of any fun, school-teacher sexiness he might have hoped for. "You're spending too much time thinking about sex and coming over here to get your rocks off to actually study."

Oh God.

*Is she breaking up with me? Really breaking up with me because of my midterm grade?*

"I swear I can do better, Ma'am." A small rebellious voice inside of him wondered when he'd ever been with a girl who gave a flying fuck about his school grades. Never. It was his own business, not hers.

But maybe he needed the firm guidance of his Domme to help him focus. He wanted to be the person he knew he could be—the sort of man who deserved to be with a woman as incredible as Victoria. Victoria already saw in him his potential—he knew she wouldn't waste her time on him if she didn't. If she thought he could do it, then he could.

So maybe…maybe she could help him buckle down and succeed.

"Please, please Ma'am, I'll do anything."

Victoria looked down at him thoughtfully. "I really am concerned that you're overstimulated. I'm going to have to think about under what conditions I can allow you back here. It sounds like you really need to focus on school right now."

"Please, Victoria," he begged. She was everything he'd ever dreamed about, and he couldn't lose her over a stupid midterm grade. "I'll study. I swear."

"You'll study and you won't have an orgasm until you bring your grades up."

"Wh-what? No orgasms, Ma'am?" he blustered. That was ridiculous. He jacked off twice a day and always had at least one incredible climax every time he visited her. And he didn't have another test for two more weeks.

"You won't come, not here and not at home. This is how I want you to submit to me. Are you strong enough to submit to me this way?"

"I...I want..." Was he strong enough to submit to her will? Damn it. For her, he'd have to be—because he wanted to be. "I want to submit to you, Ma'am, however you want me to." Oh, fuck. This was happening.

"So you won't masturbate, even if you want to. Even if you think you need to."

"I promise, Ma'am."

"If you agree to not masturbate, then I'll let you come back to see me tomorrow evening. I'll have another surprise for you that will make your abstinence much easier for you to comply with."

Well, he could promise to try not to masturbate, and if he gave in once in a while and jacked off then he'd just have another thing to confess to her. He couldn't imagine anything that would make "abstinence" easy.

Why would he even have to tell her if he masturbated? She only controlled him when he came to her door, not when he was home. Although he had to admit the idea of her long arm of dominance reaching into his everyday life was kinda hot.

"Stand up, little Blake. I'm not done with you yet. Go to the chalkboard."

* * *

Victoria had been fantasizing about having Blake handcuffed to her chalkboard ever since she ordered the thing, one of the reasons she secured two extra eyehooks on the wall by the bottom left and right corners of the board.

But all her games might come to a stop tomorrow night if he wasn't willing to submit to her plan for him. Without his full submission, she couldn't keep seeing him. A pity, too, because there was something about Blake that fulfilled a part of her she normally kept hidden from the world.

Blake stood by the chalkboard hanging on her wall, eyeing it warily.

"You'll be writing lines like the distracted school boy you are," she told him, and watched his face closely to see if his expression betrayed his thoughts on her directive. From the ever-so-slight raise of his eyebrows, she detected amusement, as if this would be a piece of cake.

Not so much.

"Pick up the chalk," she ordered.

"What do you want me to write?" He raised his arm up to start writing, probably not even noticing that with his arm stretched so high above his head he'd be tired long before he was done writing his lines. Good. She'd hung the board in the right place then.

"Write: *I won't come until my grades improve*, followed by *My cock belongs to Mistress Victori*a. 100 times, please."

Now Blake blanched noticeably. "Really?"

She smacked his already-reddened and burning hot ass cheeks with the palm of her hand before he finished his thought. "Are you asking really do I want you to write that, or really is that what's going to happen?"

He started writing quickly, his handwriting large and unsteady, probably from the difficult angle of his arm. The words, coming from him and written on the chalkboard, had the immediate effect of turning her on.

*I won't come until my grades improve. My cock belongs to Mistress Victoria. I won't come until my grades improve. My cock belongs to Mistress Victoria. I won't come until my grades improve. My cock belongs to Mistress Victoria.*

She settled back onto her bed to watch her school boy write his lines. The long, lean structure of his muscular frame, the pink bottom, and the look of worry and concentration on his face were just so perfect. She took a mental photograph of sorts to help solidify the image in her mind, to store it away in her memory bank for any time she wanted to get in the mood.

Normally she didn't insist on being called Mistress Victoria, because it didn't sound right to her for some reason. But ever since Blake had called her Ma'am the very first time he spoke to her, when he waited on her at that ridiculous diner, she'd been hooked on the show of tentative respect he gave her every time his mouth uttered that word. Seeing him write her name that way seemed fine. Looked good. Looked…hot. And making him declare her ownership over his cock was the perfect addition to the punishment for a guy who still had a rebellious streak she'd yet to train out of him.

He was slowing down now, his arm shaky with fatigue. At some point he had switched to using his left hand to write the lines, giving his handwriting a backward, slanted look to it. Awww, poor boy. Tired of writing lines. She couldn't hold back her laughter, and he looked over his shoulder at her nervously.

"Ma'am?" he asked.

"Keep going or I'll add more lines," she said sweetly.

"Yes, Ma'am."

When he finished, he put the chalk down and exhaled, stretching his overworked arms and rubbing his chalky white fingers and the muscle in between his thumb and index finger, which probably had cramped up terribly.

"Did I say you could stop?" she asked.

He froze mid-stretch. "I wrote 100 lines, Ma'am."

Victoria got off the bed, carrying two sets of handcuffs with her from her bedside table drawer. Without a word, she took his left wrist and snapped the cuff onto it and attached it to the eyehook on the wall by the bottom of the chalkboard. Seeing the other cuff in her hand, Blake offered his other wrist to her too. Such a good kid. She'd trained him well. But as she secured his right wrist to the board as well, she had to wonder. Did he really believe what she made him write on that board? Or was his submission all just a game to him?

She needed it to be real. Real submission, not just a game. And the only way to prove that to her would be for him to not get any sexual outcome from it, at least for a while. At least until he showed her that he could multi-task by doing well in school and being her submissive at the same time.

Now that Blake was cuffed to the wall with both wrists, he stared up at the words he'd written one hundred times. He sighed as if in recognition of the fact that he wasn't going to be having an orgasm for a while, unless he got his grades up.

At least, she hoped that was what his sigh was for.

"What are you waiting for?" she asked. "Clean the board."

He lifted his arm as if to rub the lines away, but of course the cuff jerked him back to place. "Ma'am?" he asked, confused.

She grinned sadistically. "Let's put that talented mouth to use, my darling Blake."

He looked at the board, the chalky white words mere inches from his face. "You want me to clean the board…"

"With your tongue," she finished the sentence for him. "Don't worry, it's non-toxic. I checked." She laughed at the look at on his face, one of lust mixed with surprise. She'd never made him do anything like this before, but she knew how much he got turned-on by unusual punishments.

"Better get started," she advised. "You're cuffed in place, so it's not like you've got any place else to be, now is there?"

Victoria smiled and settled back onto her bed to watch the show.

* * *

All Blake could taste now was the chalk in his mouth, but that wasn't the worst part. The worst part was how fucking tired his tongue was getting, and he wasn't even half-done with the huge chalkboard. Even his jaw ached as he forced himself to keep his mouth open so he could continue to lick his lines from the board.

It almost reminded him of the many times Victoria had tied him to her bed and sat on his face for as long as she wanted, which was a really long time. He loved it at the same time as he'd begun to get nervous whenever she'd straddle his head, since he knew he'd get tired long before she'd get tired. The woman was insatiable, and demanded multiple orgasms.

He jerked off to the experiences all the time, because after the fact, it was incredibly hot. Really fucking hot. But during, his tongue was a muscle after all, and that muscle got tired. He loved the feeling of having no choice, as if he had to keep going and going like the Energizer Bunny or risk her wrath.

Not that he minded her wrath. Without her punishments, he wouldn't feel so completely hers. A fleck of chalk worked its way onto the back of his tongue and he paused to swallow, but he kept cleaning the board. Victoria's punishments always surprised him with their inventiveness. He couldn't help his state of arousal, even though all he was licking was chalk and not her delicious cunt. It was the act of submitting to her that turned him on every time.

He wasn't quite done when his tongue seemed to refuse of its own accord. He kept pulling on the cuffs accidentally, trying to wipe the taste out of his mouth, as Victoria watched.

She came up behind him and he stilled his body, trying to swallow some of the white chalk dust covering his mouth. This was the hardest punishment she'd cooked up for him yet, and he wasn't even done.

To his surprise, she uncuffed his hands, and he sheepishly wiped his face with the back of his hand. "I'm sorry, Ma'am," he said, but it came out sounding weird, like he was talking through… well, a layer of chalk.

"Go rinse and wash your face," she said, not unkindly. "Are you tired yet?"

He froze on his way to her bathroom. There was no way to answer that, no way he could avoid punishment. She always did that to him, it was one of her best skills as a Domme, in his opinion. If he said he was tired, then she'd punish him. If he wasn't tired, then she'd make him finish cleaning that fucking board with his tongue. What could he say?

"Would you rather lick my pussy, or would you rather sit down and rest your mouth?" she asked.

As much as he loved the thought of licking her pussy, there was no way he was even physically capable of serving her that way at the moment. Was she really going to let him sit and rest his overworked tongue? Something wasn't right. There was no way she wasn't manipulating him, but he couldn't figure it out. What if she really wanted to let him rest before more punishment? That would be really helpful, especially since his mouth didn't seem to work at the moment. He couldn't even muster the strength to answer her, so he just stood there and looked at her.

*Can't I just go rinse?*

"Did you need me to wash your mouth out for you?" she asked sweetly, and he shook his head, knowing her way involved stinging soap. "Then hurry up."

"Yes, Ma'am," he tried to say. Sounded weird again. In the bathroom, he rinsed his mouth with cup after cup of cool water, until the chalk taste had dissipated. Amazingly, he still maintained a partial erection. Something deep inside him enjoyed licking that chalkboard clean, even one that said he wouldn't be allowed to come.

Fuck, was she serious about that?

Something told him that she was serious. But he couldn't agree to not come until his grades improved. There was no way that was even humanly possible, right?

Victoria knocked on the door to the bathroom and he opened it for her, still not trusting himself to speak without making an ass out of himself.

"All clean, dirty boy?" she asked, smiling cheerfully.

"Yes, Ma'am," he said. His words sounded clearer without the layer of chalk coating his mouth.

"Did your punishment help you learn your lesson, little Blake?"

Blake hesitated, once again unsure how to answer her. If he said it helped, then she'd use that intense punishment again. If he said it didn't help him learn his lesson, then she'd punish him more to make sure he learned it.

Fuck.

"Yes, Ma'am, it did," he finally said.

"Oh really? What lesson did you learn?"

"To not fail my midterm, Ma'am."

She laughed and shook her head. "Wrong. You definitely deserve a seat in the corner for that answer. Corner time should help you think of the right answer."

He tried not to smile so that he could look sufficiently chastised, but he couldn't help it. When Victoria had brought up corner time as a possible punishment last week, she'd watched his cock grow hard at her suggestion even as he denied that such a thing would turn him on. And his Domme never forgot things like that. She used every tool at her disposal to make their time together exactly what he needed.

Sitting on a stool in the corner should give him some time to relax before the next thing Victoria had cooked up for him. But knowing Victoria, she wasn't going to let him just sit and ponder. So what was it going to be this time?

"Come on now, we haven't got all night. Go sit down on your special seat. I really think this will help you focus."

Blake stepped out of the bathroom and walked over to the high stool she'd set in the corner of the room. He'd seen it earlier, but now, she'd affixed a huge butt plug—the kind with a suction cup base—right to the center of the seat, making it so the only way he could sit on the stool would be to impale his asshole on the plug.

"Sit," she said.

As much as the plug freaked him out, as much as he knew it would hurt going in, his traitorous cock still responded to her order with a renewed hard-on. Her amused smile showed him that his reaction hadn't escaped her notice.

Blake awkwardly tried to climb onto the stool, but it was too high up to easily sit on and also sit on the plug at the same time. The lube she'd already spread on the plug seemed to make the process even trickier, and when he finally got his balance, he sat down unexpectedly hard and fast right onto the butt plug, ramming it up his ass.

"Holy fuck!" he yelled, surprised by the force of gravity. Then, quieter, "I'm sorry, Ma'am. Ow."

"Do I have your attention now, little Blake?"

"Yes, Ma'am," he said, breathing through the pain and shock centered in his ass. The feeling started to fade a bit, so he focused on her face.

And he still had a raging hard-on.

* * *

Victoria slipped her fist around Blake's cock and squeezed. "Your cock belongs to me. That is what you were supposed to learn."

"Yes, Ma'am," he gasped.

"Do you deserve my hand on your prick, my darling?" She squeezed harder.

He shook his head no, even as he strained for more contact with her.

"I suppose not," she agreed, keeping her hand wrapped around his cock. "I suppose you don't deserve having any chance at all that you might come, not when you're just treating my apartment like a place where you can play hooky from school. You need to study, and until your grades are up, this cock is mine."

"It's always yours, Ma'am," he whispered, his face flushed from stimulation that wasn't anywhere near enough to let him have his release. "My cock belongs to you."

Wet heat flooded her panties at his words. He knew how to say exactly what she wanted to hear, and she couldn't help but to smile graciously at him before squeezing his cock again.

Blake bit his lip and she loosened her grip. The kid was a sucker for pain, and he still had an erection. "What can I do to you to make you lose this arousal?" she asked, more to think aloud than to actually glean an answer from him. "You obviously love having your ass invaded. You love it when I punish you, so punishing you won't work."

"I'm sorry, Ma'am," he said.

"I think the only way you're going to lose this erection is if you come," she sighed. "But you don't get to enjoy it, because I'm still angry with you."

Blake looked like he didn't know whether to be happy she was going to make him come, or scared that she'd do it in a way he wouldn't like.

Victoria stepped away and rummaged through her drawer. What was she going to do with him? It was obvious he didn't have the willpower to avoid masturbating on his own. He'd need a chastity device. She'd kept one from a past lover, but it was way too extreme for Blake. Blake was a guy who'd never tried to avoid getting aroused or coming, and a chastity belt covered on the inside with silicone spikes, meant to cause extreme pain if the sub even accidentally got an erection, would be way too much for him to deal with.

But the clear silicone device sat in the back of her drawer, right next to the short, suede cat-o-nine-tails whip she'd been looking for.

Would Blake even be willing to entertain the notion of a chastity belt that would punish him for getting aroused – punish him for doing anything other than study for his next test? The thought was incredibly stimulating. She'd need to orgasm herself soon, just thinking about it.

Sighing, she looked over at her naughty school boy impaled on the plug on the stool in the corner of her bedroom. It was time to take things into her own hands. The chastity device was relatively pliable silicone, made in such a way that if there were an emergency he could cut it off his cock with medical shears. Of course, she'd be pretty upset if that happened. Could she trust him to leave it on and accept the punishment? Maybe to even learn from and grow as a person from the abstinence she imposed on him?

She smacked the small suede cat-o-nine tails against her hand, reminding herself of the feel of the whip and the amount of force she should apply to her blows. When she whipped her palm softly, it felt almost like tiny tongues running over her skin. When she did it a little harder, those tongues turned to needles of pain.

Perfect.

"I'm going to whip your cock until you come," she said to Blake's back. He looked over his shoulder, and she smiled. He couldn't turn around, of course, because he was still impaled on her plug.

*Go slow. Make him sweat.*

She was champing at the bit to use her whip on his most sensitive area, but for both of their sakes she needed to retain every ounce of control.

"Well, little Blake?" she asked, stroking his cock once, feeling it throb beneath her hand. "Do you want to come, or do you want to sit here in your naughty boy corner time without any relief?"

Blake looked positively tongue-tied. "Ma'am—" He paused. "I want to come, but I'm scared of you using that on my dick." He gestured to the whip.

"Awww, this little thing?" Victoria lightly ran the suede strands of the whip over his cock, running it back and forth so he could feel the pleasure build. "This is the only way you're going to come until I say so, Blake. But if you ask me to put the whip away I will."

He breathed in sharply through clenched teeth. "Oh God, okay." Then, as if sensing that now was not the time to break decorum, he added "Ma'am."

With his full—if coerced—permission to proceed, Victoria put a little zip into her wrist movement, letting the cat-o-nine-tails sting his length just a bit. Blake gasped.

"Don't be a baby," she warned, and did it harder. Never with her full force, of course. Just enough to hurt without leaving a single mark.

"These balls," she said, grabbing his sac and gently rolling his balls in her palm, "are mine too. Just like this cock." She whipped his cock again, building a rhythm until he howled from the overstimulation.

Hot jets of thick come spurted out of his cock, and she moved her whip just in time to avoid it getting covered in his semen. As much as he probably hated having his cock whipped, he almost definitely hated having the stimulation removed just when he came. It resulted in a ruined orgasm, one that, while technically an orgasm, left the sub still feeling needy and cheated. It was a favorite trick of hers to play.

Blake gasped for breath and his cock wilted. Seizing her chance, she took the clear silicone male chastity belt with the inner spikes and slid it over his flaccid penis. She had to do it before he got hard again or the thing wouldn't go on properly.

"What the fuck?" he asked, seemingly to himself. He looked up at her with a post-climax haze.

"This is a chastity belt," she informed him, slipping the padlock through and locking it. "And this is the only key." The key was kept on a thin silver chain, which she fastened around her neck. "You, for example, do not get a key. You don't get to masturbate. You don't get to come. And in this device, you don't even get to have an erection."

* * *

Blake looked down at his locked-up cock in surprise. A fucking chastity belt? No way.

*Oh just go with it, why not?* It was surprisingly comfortable, considering he had some weird plastic thing on his dick. But no. Fuck no. Who was she to do that to him?

"You can't do this to me, Ma'am," he said firmly.

"Big words for a man sitting on a huge butt plug," she laughed. "Fine. Get off your naughty chair, go clean up, and when you come out of the bathroom I'll unlock you, if that's what you want. But you won't be invited back here again."

He paused. Really? She'd fucking break up with him over a stupid midterm grade? Actually break up with him? Fine. Fuck her.

A little voice in the back of his mind said, *It's not about the grade, it's about refusing to submit.*

Still, this wasn't what he signed up for. Letting her lock up his cock was out of the question. It was hard to make a good exit, though, with his ass impaled on the plug. He stood up on the rungs of the stool, pulling the plug out of his ass with an audible sound. It hurt like a bitch, especially the part where it got really wide, right before it narrowed to let his ass close. In the past month, she'd trained his ass to accommodate dildos bigger than most cocks, or so she loved to remind him.

It didn't matter if Victoria was the best sex he'd ever had. Didn't matter that she fulfilled something he needed, for whatever twisted reason. Stepping into the bathroom, he cleaned himself up as best he could.

The chastity belt on his limp dick was a powerful visual reminder of his submission. As much as the idea of not having access to his own cock scared him, it was the sort of adrenaline-high scare he got from watching thrillers. And he had to admit he loved the idea of only his Domme having access to his body.

*My cock belongs to Mistress Victoria.* Really? Damn it, he'd been brainwashed by all that line-writing. He'd even admitted as much to her when she had her hands on him and he could barely think straight. Was it true—did his cock really belong to her? Looking down at his locked-up cock, the answer was clear. He belonged to her, or at least his cock did.

It wouldn't be so bad, anyway. Without worrying about sex, he could really focus on studying and actually pull his grades up. Because if he thought about it, he had to admit he'd been spending way too much time playing sex games when he was supposed to be studying.

Now studying would become the new sex game, in its own way. A way of proving his submission to Victoria.

Fuck. Alright, he'd do it.

Before he lost his nerve, Blake stepped out of the bathroom. Victoria stood there with her long nails tapping the key on her neck.

"Shall I unlock you now?"

"No, Ma'am. My cock belongs to you, and if you say it has to be locked up so I can study, then that's what I'll do." The words sounded right to him, like he'd just spoken from his soul. Submitting to her felt right, too. It was a good feeling.

Victoria smiled, the sort of rare smile he worked so hard to see. It was her 'you've pleased me and I'm proud of you' smile, and whenever he saw it he fell a little bit in love with her.

"Thank you, Blake," she said. "That means a lot to me."

"It means a lot to me too, Ma'am," he admitted.

"Remember to not think about sex. Erections in that device are painful, with the hope that the pain will immediately make the erection subside. In your case, however…" her voice trailed off, but he knew what she was going to say.

He liked the pain. Pain turned him on. Hell, he just came from being whipped right on his cock. So what would happen when he got an erection? Would it hurt and that would make him even harder?

"So if you get an erection," Victoria said, "pick up a textbook and study. That's an order."

"Yes, Ma'am."

"You'll come to me every evening for five minutes only. I'll unlock you so you can check your skin for safety reasons, but then you'll be locked right back up and go home. Do you understand?"

"Yes, Ma'am." He paused. "What if I have to pee?"

"You can urinate through it, you just can't get an erection. Now get dressed and go home. You can have another orgasm only when you've proven you can get your grades up."

How was he going to that? The next test wasn't for two weeks. There was no use arguing with Victoria about it though, not if he was looking to get out of the chastity belt sooner rather than later. He might be able to beg for extra credit, but there was no guarantee the professor would go for that.

There was no way he could keep his cock locked up for too long anyway. He was used to jacking off every morning in the shower and every night before he fell asleep, at a minimum, and he'd gotten into a nice routine with Victoria of playing with her and having an orgasm from her tortuous hands or pussy at least a few times a week.

How could he survive without even being able to have a hard-on?

Fuck, he was going to get a lot of studying done.

\* \* \*

Victoria breathed a sigh of relief when he left. Thank God he hadn't decided he'd rather break up with her than submit to her. It would have been really upsetting to see him make that choice. Other subs had made that choice in the past, and it hadn't fazed her. But something about Blake was different.

She liked him.

The fact that their kinks coincided perfectly was a bonus. When they lay in bed together after sex, she often found hours would go by with them just cuddling and talking, enjoying each other's company. If he slept over, he enjoyed sleeping at the foot of the bed, like a dog. It reminded him of his place, and it kept her feet warm, since he liked to hook his arm around them and kiss her toes respectfully before finally saying goodnight and drifting off to sleep.

Sleeping with Blake every night was something she could get used to—but only if he could be completely submissive to her will.

Tonight, he'd proven he could, and would.

Any other night she would have ended his punishment by Queening him, sitting on his face with his hands tied up above his head. She loved to sit on his mouth and nose and watch as he grew increasingly nervous, with her not moving until he licked her even faster, and then she'd reward him by letting him breathe as he licked her pussy. Exerting that kind of power over such a strong man brought on her climax just as much as his tongue did.

But since he always got an erection when she did that to him, she let him off easy by sending him home without pleasuring her. In its own way, watching his punishment—

the paddling, writing lines, cleaning the chalkboard, the naughty chair—all of that was almost pleasure enough.

Almost. She still needed to come, or she'd have that uncomfortable feeling in her groin, that feeling that most guys referred to as blue balls. Women could get that too, she knew from experience. Except it would be her clit that would get all swollen and horny, and without release she'd just have to wait for the blood flow to her groin to dissipate.

Blake was going to be feeling that a lot in the next few days. The thought of his cock locked up even from himself made her panties dampen.

*I need to come, with or without Blake's help.*

She lay back on her bed and pulled her trusty dildo out of her bedside table. The pink toy with the vibrating bunny ears that flicked over her clit while the dildo rolled and rotated inside of her was one of her favorites. Slipping it deep inside her wet cunt, Victoria set the vibrating bunny ears on high and thought about Blake lying over her lap, his spank-reddened ass cheeks seeming to beg for more punishment.

*You've been a bad, bad, boy.*

She thought about Blake getting hard, the silicone spikes lining the chastity belt sticking him, making him cry out in pain as he tried to force himself to calm down, to follow her orders. The thought of his face, filled with fear and panic and pain all mixed with desire—a look she aspired to see on him at least once every few dates—brought her climax crashing down on her.

The sound of her panting breath filled the room, and she cried out, her head snapping up toward her belly as she rode the wave of her orgasm. Finally, the aftershocks subsided, and she closed her eyes to focus on the warm, tingly feeling of post-orgasmic bliss.

Still, a part of her wished Blake had been the one to make her come.

*I think I'm getting attached to him.*

Damn it.

\* \* \*

The first night with the chastity belt sucked. Blake woke up every few hours with a nocturnal erection and had to breathe through the pain of the spikes digging into his tender flesh, until he was able to lose the erection and fall back asleep. He wasn't even purposefully trying to get hard, but it was happening anyway, and in his sleep too. It almost didn't seem fair that he should be punished for hard-ons he didn't even want.

He woke up an hour early for work at the diner with another erection and gasped. Fuck, this was not going to work.

*Pick up a text book,* Victoria had said. *Study.*

Sighing, Blake got out of bed and grabbed one of his textbooks, the most boring one he could find, motivated solely by his cock being on fire from the pain. He needed to lose this erection ASAP.

Settling into his desk chair, he pushed aside the papers and random shit covering the surface of his desk and set the textbook down.

It wasn't nearly as boring as he'd remembered it to be, for some reason. His cell-phone alarm rang an hour later, the time he'd normally be getting up, and it felt like only moments had gone by. No more erection, either.

*Holy shit, this is working.*

He went through the rest of the day at work without too many problems, either. The occasional half-hard-on while he daydreamed about Victoria punished him with immediate consequences in that damn chastity belt. He hadn't even realized how often he'd slip into a fantasy during the day. Knowing he couldn't afford to slack off and let his mind wander, Blake spent his time being super attentive to his customers and pulled in the best tips he'd ever gotten. Ever.

Well, unless you count the spanking Victoria gave him in lieu of a tip. That might still be the best one.

He stopped at her place after work as promised, but she gave him an icy, business-like reception.

"Come in," she said, and he stepped into her living room, closing the door to her apartment behind him.

She gestured toward the ground. "Drop your pants." Lifting her glossy burgundy painted fingernails to the latch on her necklace, she quickly produced the key for his chastity belt and handed it to him. "Do it yourself, you don't get to have my hands on you—not yet."

Blake's cheeks felt hot as he unlocked the padlock securing the chastity belt. Free now, his cock immediately hardened, as if it had been trained to respond to her presence.

*It had.*

"Check your skin. Look for red marks from the chastity belt, any pressure areas, that sort of thing."

His skin looked fine. After the way the spikes had been torturing him, he'd imagined his dick might be in the process of falling off. But no, he was fine.

"Lift your balls, look all over."

Everything was fine. It was good, he supposed, but now that meant she had no reason not to keep him locked up, unable to even masturbate.

Victoria sighed. "You need to get rid of your erection if you're going to get that thing back on."

*Yes!* Maybe he'd get to come after all.

She laughed. "I know what you're thinking. Next time bring your textbook with you so you can study."

"But, this time? Ma'am?" *Please,* he pleaded with his eyes.

She pointed to the dreaded Welcome mat she kept just inside her doorway. It was one of those spiky plastic ones meant for scraping mud off of your boots, and she loved to make him sit or kneel on it until he was begging for mercy. "Sit," she said. "You can read this manuscript until you go limp, and then I'll lock you back up."

"Manuscript?" He knew she was an editor, but she didn't talk much about her work.

"It's particularly boring. Hopefully boring enough to make you lose your erection."

She was right, of course. Less than ten minutes later, his cock was locked back inside the chastity belt and she shooed him out the door.

But that night, alone in his room, he couldn't help but think about her—and her spankings and punishments and hell, even the plastic Welcome mat—and get aroused. He studied for hours until he fell asleep.

He awoke with a painful erection and a burning desire to come. *Please, Victoria.* He imagined himself calling her and begging her to set him free so he could masturbate. *Just once. I need to come.*

But he couldn't do that, it wouldn't be submitting to her will. Victoria ordered that he couldn't come until his grades improved, and what she said was law. She made the rules, and that was how he liked it. If he didn't, then he wouldn't be with her.

Still, he felt like he had to keep reminding himself that he was doing this for her, and ultimately for himself. That having multiple daily orgasms was overrated if he couldn't even pass a fucking junior college English Lit class. Right?

Right.

By the time the weekend rolled around, Blake had not only been studying his ass off, but he'd spoken to his professor about doing some extra credit. She'd given him an insanely difficult assignment, but she did give him one, and that was exactly what he needed. The A-minus she'd given him on it would raise his overall grade to passing at least, and hopefully that meant Victoria would allow him out of the chastity belt for longer than a quick once-over of his skin...and let him back into her bed.

His phone rang just as he got out of the shower while preparing to go to Victoria's apartment. 'Preparing' meant getting cleaned out with one of those drugstore enemas that came in a three pack. He'd gotten to the point where just seeing an enema bottle made him think of all the things Victoria might do to him later that night, and he'd get a hard-on, just from looking at the fucking thing. Tonight, of course, that meant turning his shower to freezing cold and jumping in so he'd lose his erection quickly.

His Mistress was diabolical. She'd even gotten him punishing himself on his own time, it seemed.

It was Victoria on the phone. "Do we need to cancel our date so you can study, or have you managed to get your grades up?" she asked without preamble.

"My grades are better, Ma'am," he said, dropping his towel on the carpet in the bedroom so that the cool air on his dripping wet skin would make him too shiver-y to get hard.

"Great! See you soon. You're going to come so hard tonight, and I promise it will feel incredible."

Ahh fuck. And now he was hard again. Diabolical, evil genius, that's what his Mistress was. Surely she called him on purpose, for some last-minute agony before the pleasure.

Wait a minute. When had she ever promised him pleasure before? Usually the pleasure she gave him came from the pleasure he got from serving her or submitting to her. Something was up. What would happen when he got to her apartment? Knowing Victoria like he did, something told him that when she promised him that something would "feel incredible," that might mean…

*Oh God, what did that mean?*

\* \* \*

Blake stood in front of apartment 4C in Victoria's building, holding the extra-credit essay he'd written with the purple A-minus scrawled across the top. He wasn't sure if she'd ask for proof before letting him come, and he didn't want to risk her turning him away.

A man answered the door. *What the fuck?* What was another man doing at her apartment? Waves of jealousy rode through him immediately.

The man was shorter than Blake, and leaner, with a collar around his neck and nothing on but a pair of tightie-whities, through which the man's dick was stretching the material considerably.

"Hello, Blake," he said warmly. "I'm Jesse."

Victoria's voice behind him interrupted. "Jesse, let him come in before I call your Mistress and tell her you've forgotten your manners."

Jesse grinned as if he liked that idea, and gestured Blake inside.

Blake stood in the entranceway, his back to the door, still completely confused. Victoria looked incredible in a tightly-laced black corset and boots. *Don't get distracted.*

"Who is this guy?" he demanded.

Victoria laughed. "Jealous, are you? That's so cute. But you have no territorial rights over me, as I'm sure you must realize."

"I don't want to be with someone who's fucking other guys," he said, forgetting to call her Ma'am, forgetting everything except his primal instinct to claim her as *his* woman, when all this time he'd been hoping she'd claim him as her man.

Her smile fell from her beautiful face, and she looked directly at him. "I'm not fucking anyone, including you. We can discuss our relationship's boundaries some other time, if you'd like. For now, all you need to know is that the lovely Jesse here—" she gestured to the man in the collar and tightie-whities—"is on loan to me from one of my girlfriends, Mistress Lori. She's training her husband in the art of oral sex, and I told her I knew of a naughty young man who might need his cock sucked."

"H-husband?" Blake looked at the dude who opened the door in a new light. That was someone's husband? Did people play these games for real, all the time? Did they—could they—get married and live together as Mistress and slave?

*Fuck, it looked like they could.*

The revelation opened a whole new level of possibility to his world. If this was his kink, if this was what made him happy, then why settle for a vanilla wife he'd fuck twice a week and make 1.5 babies with and live in suburbia when he could have… a collar?

Victoria interrupted his train of thought by handing him the key to his chastity belt. "Strip," she said, and he did. "I'm proud of you for bringing your grades up," she offered him his favorite smile—her *I approve* smile. "And as a reward, you're going to get your cock sucked."

Blake's cock jumped to attention as soon as he slipped the silicone chastity belt off, as if his body heard and responded to the words "cock sucked" even when his brain knew she was talking about having this other guy do it.

"I'm not sure I'm comfortable with that, Ma'am," he said, a common mantra for him, something he found himself saying when she'd tease him about licking up his own come or about taking something up his ass. "Please, I don't want a dude to suck my dick."

"Really?" she asked, pointing at his rock-hard erection. "Tell your gorgeous cock that."

"Ma'am," he whispered, not wanting to offend Jesse, who watched the exchange from the corner, standing patiently, waiting to learn how to become an oral sex expert for his wife.

"If you don't want to come, then you may put the chastity belt back on and come back next week, when we'll try this again. I'm sure Mistress Lori's slave will accommodate your schedule." She turned to Jesse. "You'll be able to come back next week to suck Blake's cock, won't you?"

"Yes, Mistress Victoria," Jesse said, coloring slightly.

*Ah fuck. That dude's not gay either. He's like me. He gets off on submitting, and sucking my cock is submitting to his Mistress.*

Blake paused. Guess that meant that getting his cock sucked by this slave was going to be Blake's way of submitting, at least for now.

And he desperately wanted to come. His cock ached it was so hard. A drop of pre-come moistened the tip.

"Well, little Blake? Will you take your reward or would you prefer to torture yourself for another week of chastity?"

"Yes, Ma'am. I'll...take my reward."

She laughed. "You'll have to ask Jesse here if he's willing to suck you off."

Blake swallowed hard. "Um, Jesse, are you willing?"

The dude nodded and kneeled before him, and Blake looked down at his shaved head and masculine shoulders. There was no way he'd be able to come from a dude blowing him. That just wasn't what he was into, not at all.

"Say please. Tell him you want it," Victoria ordered.

"Please," he said. "I...I want it." His balls started to ache and he knew he was about two seconds from begging for this guy to put his mouth on him.

Jesse put his mouth on his tip and Blake closed his eyes, determined to imagine the slave blowing him was Victoria, her deep red lips wrapped around his shaft...

"Open your eyes," she ordered. "You have a very handsome man sucking your cock, and I want you to watch every second so you can truly appreciate that."

Blake groaned in frustration, watching the man on his knees working his cock deeper into his throat, gagging but not stopping. Why did this have to feel so fucking good? If he enjoyed it, what did that say about him?

"His cock looks so hot thrusting down your throat, Jesse," Victoria murmured to her friend's husband, and for some reason, those words combined with Jesse's mouth on his cock made him explode in the guy's mouth.

"Keep sucking," he heard himself say. "Please…please…swallow it."

The slave listened, and swallowed every last drop of his come, even going as far as licking his shaft and balls clean with his tongue after. It was an incredible feeling—no wonder Victoria liked the power of having a submissive man at her feet.

She smiled at him. "Nicely done, both of you. You are dismissed," she said to Jesse, and he dressed quickly, throwing a pair of khaki pants on over the impressive bulge in his tight white underwear, and left. Presumably to go home to his Mistress/Wife.

Blake took a few deep breaths, still recovering from the mind-blowing orgasm he'd just experienced. Not coming for over a week made that climax one of the strongest he'd ever had—and at the hands—well, mouth—of another dude. Fuck.

Victoria wrapped her arms around his neck and kissed his lips, something she rarely did, and only when she was feeling particularly pleased with him. He pulled her in close, kissing her back, and dropping his lips to her neck, to her cleavage, which peeked out the top of her tight black corset.

"That really turned me on, watching the slave suck your cock," she murmured. "I'm so wet for you, Blake."

"May I have the honor of pleasuring you, Ma'am?" He lifted her small frame in his arms and placed her on the couch, settling down between her legs.

She moaned as he pushed her panties to one side so he could access her labia and sweet clit. With long, leisurely strokes, he licked her pussy and sighed with contentment.

This was where he belonged. This was the life he wanted, not just now, but forever.

"I want to be yours, Victoria," he breathed against her thigh. "Yours alone."

"That means being my collared slave," she said, spreading her legs wider to give him better access to her dripping cunt.

"I don't know if you're ready for that. If you even know what that would mean, to be my permanent, live-in slave."

"Teach me."

Victoria tucked her finger under his chin and lifted his head from between her thighs. She smiled. "I will."

*The End*

# IN HER CARE: NOVELLA 3

Victoria Sanders smiled down at the handsome, naked young man she'd been seeing for the past six months, hoping he wouldn't notice her hands trembling as she opened the black bag. Blake knelt before her, a matching smile on his face.

This was a big moment, the point in a relationship that she never dreamed she'd get to experience. The thin leather collar she produced from the bag signified her commitment to her sub, her commitment to guide him and to dominate him. Blake was moving into her apartment, and while he'd continue to go to school and work at the diner where they'd met, serving as her full-time slave would be his first priority.

This was her first full-time live-in slave, actually. The mere thought of it made her panties damp. Sure, she'd had lovers in the past who'd enjoyed the occasional game where she'd get the chance to play Dominatrix, but at the end of the day those men wanted to make their own choices and decisions. They wanted to be in charge of *her* at all times except in the bedroom. No way. She couldn't settle for less than what she truly needed to be content: a man who was willing to submit to her fully. All the time.

Could Blake be that man?

Time would tell. She'd have to make the first week or two extra difficult for him, so she'd know early on if he was going to reneg on her and want out of their contract.

*Their contract.* Reading that contract out loud to him had her so hot she had to force herself not to climb on top of his face right then and there. The contract said she owned him. That he was her property to do with as she pleased. If she wanted to use him as a dishwasher, or a footstool, or a sex toy, she could. He was hers. If she wanted to lock up his cock again in a chastity belt the way she did when he needed to focus on his school work, she could. If she decided he needed to be whipped or spanked or sent to the naughty corner to sit on a huge butt plug and think about what he did, then she could.

He was hers.

"Blake, do you understand what this collar means?" she asked, wrapping the leather around his neck. She paused before slipping the padlock into place, waiting for his final permission.

"Yes, Ma'am."

"You choose to be my collared slave. Once you choose that, it's the last choice you get to make. I'll own you. Do you understand?"

Was that hesitation she saw? A flicker of uncertainty crossing his face? Good. He needed to think long and hard about what he was offering her by giving her the gift of his full submission. She'd heard it termed consensual non-consent, and that would seem fitting, if he didn't have a history of always willingly—eagerly—going along with her games.

"Yes, Ma'am. I'm yours."

She clicked the padlock into place and put the key onto her necklace. "You're mine."

Blake looked so sexy kneeling naked on the floor of her bedroom, his cock saluting her. Apparently giving up his freedom turned him on as much as making him her slave turned her on. She leaned down and kissed his lips, an act she reserved for special occasions. This occasion definitely warranted a kiss.

"Thank you, Ma'am," he whispered, and she kissed him once more.

"What shall I do with you on your first night as my official slave?" she wondered aloud. Thank goodness it was Friday night, so she could do with him as she pleased and not worry about him having to study. She had some manuscripts she had to get through, but for now all she wanted to do was bask in her new position as Mistress.

"I think we should have a little party to celebrate," she announced. She'd already invited a couple over to meet her slave, though Blake didn't know it yet. These friends had been itching for a chance to get to know Blake ever since she told them about him.

It would be the perfect opportunity to test Blake's willingness to submit to her will. Sure, he was okay with her doing things to him, but would he be willing to let her power extend to her lending him out? If she owned him like he said she did, then he should want to do as she said. Besides, Blake was so easy to read. His dick did all the talking. Even though he sometimes protested a punishment, his erection would give him away. It was if he wanted to be "forced" to submit, sometimes.

Other times, he'd go out of his way to prove how much he wanted to serve her. That was nice. But pushing his limits, making him beg and making him question his submission—that was what really got her hot.

And if his hard cock told the truth, then that was what got Blake hot too.

\* \* \*

Blake looked up at Victoria, his heart racing with adrenaline. It was happening—he'd finally become her full-time slave. Just being able to live in the same apartment as her was going to be awesome. They'd get to play all the time now—even if playing meant he'd be cleaning her bathroom while she relaxed.

Yeah, he was down for it. Cleaning wasn't his thing, but doing something—anything—for Victoria certainly was. No other woman made him feel the way she did.

And no other woman loved to punish him as much as she did. That alone made her basically perfect for him. Most women didn't understand why a grown man might want to be spanked or even really hurt. The few girls he'd dated who he'd tried to play games with weren't into it, or thought it was silly.

Not Victoria. She took their games to a whole other level. A level where…it wasn't even a game anymore.

"Well?" she said, snapping her fingers as she turned and walked out of the bedroom. He dropped to his hands and knees and followed her down the hard, wood-floored hallway that led to her living room. "Are you up for some company?"

"Yes, Ma'am," he replied. "Whatever you want, Ma'am."

"Good boy. I'm going to remind you of that later."

*Fuck.* What on earth did that mean? Was it going to be that slave and his Wife, the Dominatrix who sent her husband over in a collar (and not much else) to suck Blake's cock so the slave could "learn how to be an oral sex expert," as Victoria had bluntly put it?

Blake wasn't sure he'd be able to look that guy in the face and not blush. For one, neither that guy nor Blake was actually into dudes. But they were both so into their Mistresses that—that night at least—they were willing to do whatever they were told.

Fuck.

The doorbell rang. His first instinct was to open the door, to act as a butler of sorts for his Mistress. But he was naked and wearing a collar…should he be answering the door like that? He looked at Victoria for an order.

"What are you waiting for? Answer the door, little Blake. Invite our guests inside."

"Yes, Ma'am." He paused with his hand on the doorknob. "Ma'am? Should I maybe get some pants on first?"

Victoria laughed and shook her head. "Don't keep them waiting."

Blake took a deep breath for courage and opened the door, his traitorous cock rising to half-mast.

*Please don't be the dude who sucked me off.*

"You must be Blake," a sweet, feminine voice said.

The young woman was beautiful, in a completely different way from Victoria's beauty. Victoria was pale with dark hair and a penchant for black leather and latex. This pretty thing at the door was tan and blonde and looked like she came straight from Malibu Barbie's playhouse.

"Um, y-yes," he stuttered. She stood there waiting patiently until he laughed with embarrassment and backed out of the entranceway so she could come inside.

"I'm Sandy," she said. To Victoria, she added, "Tom is parking the car. It's impossible to find a spot in Midtown, you know how it is."

"That's why I'm grateful I have a parking garage," Victoria said. "May I take your coat?"

Sandy blushed, and before Blake's eyes, she seemed to morph into a sub. "Yes, Mistress Victoria, but I'm not wearing anything underneath it. Tom's orders."

"I see," she murmured. "Well, no reason we shouldn't get this party started then, right? Drop the coat."

Sandy looked at Blake and shrugged with a laugh, as if to say "Dommes, can't live with 'em, can't top from the bottom." She dropped her coat to the carpet, revealing a curvy physique complete with bikini tan lines. A silver chain with a padlock adorned her slender neck.

"What a pretty little slave you are, Sandy," Victoria said. "What else did your Master order you to do?"

Sandy giggled nervously, even though it seemed she and Victoria had played together before. Where? At a BDSM club? At a party? Had Victoria been doing stuff without him in the past six months they'd been dating? The thought brought with it simmering jealousy, an uncomfortable emotion he'd hoped would go away once he had her collar on his neck for reassurance.

"Um, he ordered me to lick your boot, Mistress."

"Well?"

Sandy got down on her knees and pressed her lips to Victoria's tall black leather stiletto-heeled boot. Blake watched in fascination as her pink tongue darted out her mouth and licked enthusiastic swirls all over Victoria's boot.

His Mistress caught him staring and heat flushed through his face. He didn't want Victoria to think he was interested in anyone but her.

"Do you like Sandy's tongue, little Blake?"

*Fuck!* Trick question—it had to be. If he said yes, would Victoria be jealous or angry? If he said no, was he insulting her guest? His Mistress had perfected the fine art of throwing him into a state of panic on an hourly basis.

"I'm yours, Ma'am," he said carefully. Sandy stopped licking Victoria's boot and sat on her haunches, watching the exchange with interest. Someone knocked on the door.

"My Master's here, Mistress Victoria," Sandy said.

"Get the door, Blake," Victoria ordered. He walked over to the door, once again reminded of his complete nudity. What would the man, this stranger, think of him?

It didn't even matter, since only his Mistress's opinion mattered to him.

And he liked it that way, so fuck feeling embarrassed about being naked and collared in front of strangers. If he was going to be Victoria's full-time slave then he'd better get used to the idea.

He opened the door and smiled, determined to greet this Dom properly. "Hello, Sir."

"Howdy there, Blake," the man said, grinning affably. He wore jeans and a flannel shirt and a cowboy hat, an outfit that was almost inconceivable in New York City. Howdy? Did people actually talk like that?

Victoria hugged the man Sandy called Tom like he was her long-lost friend. Maybe he was. "It's so good to see you," she gushed. "How long are you in town?"

"We're fixin' to stay as long as I need to get a deal closed, but then I'll be ready to quit the city and go back to our home sweet home."

Hmm. A business man? He looked like a fucking farmer. But maybe he was some millionaire ranch guy or some shit like that. Whoever he was, he didn't fit in here in Manhattan, that was for sure.

"My slave was just trying to tell me that he had no interest in your slave's tongue," Victoria said, laughing. "Do you think he's telling the truth?"

"Only one way to find out," Tom said. Then he looked at Blake and grinned sadistically. "Let's have ourselves a little wager."

Blake swallowed hard and stayed silent. Sandy looked positively excited, her eyes gleaming as she looked at Tom. Then again, she was probably familiar with her Dom's methods, whereas Blake was definitely not. Which was scary.

Tom looked over at Victoria. "Can I do what I want with him?"

"What's mine is yours," she said sweetly.

*Wait, what?* She was lending him to the huge Dom—the fucking cowboy?

"Sandy here is gonna use her tongue to lick your asshole for me. And if you don't like her tongue, and you don't like people messing with your cute butt there, then you won't be getting' an erection." Tom grinned and Blake felt shivers of terror mixed with dark lust run down his spine. But why lust, for a man, when Blake knew in his soul that he was only interested in Victoria?

Because Victoria had given him to this Dom, so he had no choice but to submit to his domination. And there was something about that situation that turned him on like crazy. Dear God, what was wrong with him?

Sandy hurried over to Blake and stood behind him.

"Hurry up," Victoria said. "Don't keep Tom waiting once he's told you what to do. I'm watching you, Blake. If you're naughty don't think I won't notice. Don't think I won't start off your collaring with you being tied down and whipped till every inch of skin on your body has a welt mark on it." She looked pointedly at his cock, which was at half-mast, as if it couldn't decide whether to get hard or to shrink back like a turtle head from fear. "And I do mean every single inch will be whipped."

Blake nodded, bent forward and grabbed his ankles—the position Victoria favored when she wanted access to his anus. He felt Sandy's warm hands spread his ass cheeks and her breath on his sensitive skin.

He'd licked Victoria's asshole plenty of times, since she liked to sit on his face backwards while she raked her fingernails over his balls. If he stopped licking, she'd pinch until he started again, something he both dreaded and got excited over. But…he'd never had his own ass tongued before.

"Wait," Tom's voice came from somewhere above him. "I didn't tell you the wager. The best part."

*If this Dom is anything like my Domme, there is no way I'm gonna win this bet.*

"If you really aren't into it, then you don't get hard, no harm no foul. You'll get to fuck Sandy's tight pussy if you don't get hard. But Sandy doesn't like anyone's cock in her unless it's her Master's, ain't that right, baby?"

"Yes, Sir," she said, her mouth still inches away from Blake's asshole.

"So I have a feelin' that Sandy's gonna try real hard to get you to like her tongue, now ain't you baby?"

Sandy giggled. "Yes, Sir."

"But if you like it," Tom continued, "if your prick gets hard, then I'm gonna ass fuck you like you've never been fucked before."

Blake mouth dropped open. He shut his mouth quickly, hoping no one had noticed his reaction, and bit his lip. He'd never had sex with a man before. Well, except for when that male slave blew him. But to actually get fucked in the ass by a male Dom? Holy shit.

Just six months ago he would have called out his safeword, stood up and gone home at the mere threat of getting fucked in the ass by a man. But now…

He looked over at his Mistress, the woman he'd do anything for. Victoria smiled and nodded. "Don't be so scared, little Blake. I've fucked you with huge dildos and butt plugs, now haven't I?"

"Yes, Ma'am." She had. And some of those were way bigger than any man's cock could be. So it wasn't like he hadn't had any anal training.

Had she been preparing him for something like this all along?

"Go on, Sandy," Victoria urged. "I want to watch my slave try not to get hard." She laughed mercilessly, as if she knew there was no way in hell he'd be able to not get an erection with a hot girl gently laving his most sensitive nerve-endings.

Sandy's hot wet tongue licked his asshole and he tried to not feel it, tried to pretend it wasn't happening. If he could just forget about her then he could fuck her soon. He could fuck the slave's hot pussy—*ahhh shit* he was getting hard.

*Stop! Think of something else.* Sandy stuck the tip of her tongue into his asshole, darting it in and out, fucking him with her mouth. It felt so good. *No!*

He had plenty of practice when it came to forcing himself to not get hard. When Victoria put him in a male chastity belt lined with silicone spikes, every hard-on was pure torture. To get rid of the pain, he'd do anything—from jumping into a freezing cold shower to picking up the most complicated, boring textbook he owned and actually studying.

Sandy's tongue swirled around the sensitive nerve endings of his ass and he gripped his ankles hard, feeling unsteady all of a sudden, like he might fall over. He had a test in school next week in his statistics class. If he could just recall some of the information he'd been studying for that test, he could take his mind off of sex and not get hard…

Suddenly Sandy's hot little tongue was gone. "I'm sorry Tom," she said. "I swear I did my best to get Mistress Victoria's slave ready for you."

Tom laughed and lifted Blake to standing by grabbing his ear playfully. "Look at you, winning our wager. Now you get to fuck Sandy's cunt, you lucky boy you."

Blake looked over at Victoria in surprise. Would she be okay with that? "Ma'am?"

Victoria stood from the couch and pointed to the floor. "Lie on your back. Sandy can ride you while I sit on your face and watch."

*Fuck yeah.*

But wait—Blake looked at Sandy, watching her face carefully. "If you don't want to, I understand. It's okay."

"You don't get it, do you?" Sandy asked, a smile still on her lips. The same lips that had been on his ass just a moment before. "I belong to Tom. What he says goes. If he says I'm going to fuck you, then I'm going to fuck you—and I'm going to love every second of it."

"But—I just meant—he said you didn't like to fuck other guys. Other than him, I mean."

"I'm going to love every second of it because I love obeying Tom."

Huh. That made sense to him, actually.

Blake lay on the carpet, feeling the plush fibers press against his naked skin. From his position on the floor, everyone appeared so tall and in control, even Sandy. She stroked her manicured hand reverently over his cock, and just that movement on his shaft had him hard. This time he didn't try to thwart nature.

"Go on girl, fuck 'em good," Tom said, and Sandy sheathed Blake's cock with a condom before straddling him and guiding him into her pussy.

Pure velvet heat clasped his cock as she rode him, throwing her blonde hair back over her shoulder and sliding her cunt up and down his shaft.

With Sandy straddling his legs so she could fuck his cock, Victoria straddled his head so he could eat her pussy. The familiar scent of his Mistress's shrine made him buck his hips, trying to fuck Sandy harder. He sucked Victoria's clit into his mouth and worked it around with his tongue and lips, not even caring that he could barely breathe beneath the weight of her thighs and ass on his face.

If he died like this, he'd die a happy man.

He grabbed Sandy's hips and thrust hard inside her, taking control of the ride even as Victoria clenched her thighs harder around his face, forcing him even closer to her cunt, which he licked fervently. He never got to be the one controlling the sex with Victoria, and he didn't mind at all— but being able to fuck this slave girl's pussy as hard as he wanted, knowing she loved it because her Dom was watching and approving—holy fuck.

He slammed hard into Sandy's cunt, loving her short, gasping moans. Victoria reached down and grabbed his hair where it brushed against her inner thigh. Her fingernails tugged on his scalp, her pussy grinding against his mouth.

"Listen to me, little Blake," Victoria said, her voice breathless above him. He tried to distance himself from the pleasure of fucking Sandy so he could concentrate on his Mistress's words.

"Yes, Ma'am," he said, the sound muffled against her cunt.

"When you feel like you might die, bite the inside of my thigh."

When he felt like he might *die*? What on earth—oh fuck. Victoria shifted her weight, relaxing back onto his face, covering his nose and mouth completely with her pussy and ass. He struggled to take in a breath and couldn't.

*Oh fuck, I really can't breathe this time. They'll have to put death by pussy on my tombstone.*

"I'm not moving until you make me come," Victoria said.

Lust flowed through him at her words. This was exactly what he loved the most—being completely at the mercy of his lovingly sadistic Dominatrix. Serving her, giving her pleasure at his own expense—that was all he wanted in life.

Blake licked as fast as he could, suckling her clit and moving his mouth up and down, trying to build a rhythm so she should come.

"I could fuck your mouth till you pass out," she warned, and Blake moaned and did his best with his tongue, feeling the panic of oxygen deprivation now. He should bite her thigh, but he didn't want to fail her. He had to make her come.

Images flashed through his mind, the edges of his reality getting blurry. He pictured his Mistress whipping him, he pictured her riding him the way Sandy was riding him right now…a flash of very recent memory popped in—Victoria placing the collar on him, claiming him as her own. Bright lights spotted his vision behind his closed eyelids, his mouth working hard, sucking her clit, even as he tried to draw a breath against her cunt and only got another mouthful of succulent flesh.

Fuck. He bit the inside of her thigh, hard, and she moaned and came, a gush of fluid covering his mouth. Victoria shifted back, allowing him some air, and he took in a deep breath, gasping greedily for air before diving back into his Mistress's shrine. As he lapped up her juices, Sandy kept pumping him, riding his body. He'd been so wrapped up in Victoria's orgasm that he'd almost been able to forget about his own.

Almost.

Victoria climbed off his face and sat next to his head, staring down at him, watching him fuck this slave girl. "Go on Blake, you can come now."

Blake grabbed the girl's hips and lifted her up and down his shaft, feeling the slide of her pussy against his length. She was so wet, so hot…he exploded inside her, his climax coming on so fast he nearly screamed with ecstasy as he finished spurting inside the condom.

He laid his head back and grinned, looking up at Sandy. But Sandy was still going, grinding her clit against his cock, even though he'd lost his erection and had fallen out from inside her.

"You're hurting me, Sandy," he said.

Her clit rubbing against his over-stimulated post-orgasmic cock felt like she was trying to torture him. As soon as the words came out of his mouth, he realized she probably was. Just as he never got the chance to fuck a woman hard like that, she was probably using her opportunity to play with a male slave as well.

"I wanna come," she said. "So you just keep right on lying there, looking pretty." Sandy giggled and continued to rub her clit as fast as she could on his cock, bouncing on him like he was a carnival ride.

\* \* \*

"How's that feel, little Blake?" Victoria asked, amused. Watching the two subs try to top each other was adorable. Watching her own sub lie on the floor, his over-stimulated cock being punished by another woman rubbing her clit on him, was sexy beyond all hell.

"I think you like torturing my little slave, don't you, Sandy?" she asked.

Sandy giggled. "I do," she admitted.

"Watch out, Tom, you might have a switch on your hands."

Sandy laughed, and kept rubbing on Blake's wilted cock. His face, a mix of agony and lust, was priceless.

"Sandy, would you like to spank my slave for me?"

Sandy stopped grinding and looked up at her Dom for permission.

"Go ahead, darlin' the boy looks like he could use a spanking," Tom answered.

She smiled down at Blake mischievously and rubbed her clit even harder against him, throwing her head back in ecstasy. "Just you wait...I'm gonna spank you so hard," she gasped, climaxing, as if getting that permission from her Dom had thrown her over the edge.

"This is so much fun," Sandy laughed, jumping up to her feet. "I've never gotten to spank anyone before."

Blake looked at her warily, but he stood up as well.

"What are you doing?" Victoria asked him. She loved the look of confusion on his face as he swayed on his feet for a moment, as if unsure of what to do. "Get on your knees and follow Sandy like a proper slave. I've loaned you to her for your maintenance spanking."

Blake dropped down to all fours and followed them as they walked down the hallway into the bedroom. Victoria could barely wait. The idea of watching someone else punish her slave was so enticing, she was wet just thinking about it.

When they got into the bedroom, Victoria looked around at the various schoolroom props she had—the naughty chair for corner time, the chalkboard for writing lines, the school desk for being bent over and paddled. But no, none of those would do right now. Now, it was time for some old-fashioned spanking.

"Sit, dear," she said to Sandy, and pointed to the wooden chair situated by the foot of the bed. Sandy complied, a nervous grin on her face. "And you, you naughty boy, over her lap."

Blake quickly laid himself over the woman's lap, his torso supported by the end of the bed. He laid his cheek on the soft purple duvet and looked at Victoria.

"Is everything okay, little Blake? You look...scared. Are you scared of a little hand spanking from another slave?"

Blake froze, and Victoria laughed, knowing she'd confused him again. If he said he wasn't scared, then he knew she'd make sure this would be a spanking to remember. If he said he *was* scared, well, then...he was admitting to being a scared young man instead of the tough guy he loved to pretend to be. A tough guy who licked his Mistress's boot on command.

"Well?" she probed. Sandy was rubbing his bottom, something she probably picked up from her own experiences over Tom's knee.

"I'm okay, Ma'am," he finally said.

"Very well." She turned to Sandy. "Why don't you do to Blake what your Master does to you when you're naughty? What's the worst spanking he's given you? Do that to my little Blake here."

Sandy blushed. "The very worst spanking involved raw ginger," she said, looking up at her Dom, who smiled as if remembering his sub with a raw ginger fig up her ass, squirming from the searing burn of it as he spanked her. "I don't suppose you have any ginger?" she asked hopefully.

"No, dear, no ginger this time."

"That's okay," Sandy said. "I can dole it out pretty good, I think." She brought her hand down on Blake's ass hard, no warm up, and Blake jumped a bit. Her hand made a satisfying slapping sound.

"Tom doesn't warm up my ass when I'm really naughty," she explained, and spanked Blake again. "And he does this." She spanked a bunch of times fast, in one spot, right on his sit spot—where he'd have no choice but to sit tomorrow, and where he'd surely be reminded of this spanking. "It hurts when I keep spanking the same spot, doesn't it, slave?" she asked Blake.

Blake had buried his face in the duvet, probably to keep from squealing like a pig. He had to turn his head to answer her.

"Yes, it hurts."

Sandy moved to the other cheek and repeated the spanking, over and over on one spot. Blake gritted his teeth.

"Tom doesn't stop, not for the longest time," Sandy said, and kept on going. Blake's ass was turning a beautiful shade of red.

Victoria smiled at Tom. "She likes being on the other side of the hand, it seems."

Tom laughed. "She'll get her own spanking when we get home to remind her who's boss, won't you, darlin'?"

Sandy smiled and paused. "Yes, thank you Sir," she answered, and kept on spanking.

Victoria couldn't keep still, her own labia and clit felt swollen and wet and ready for action. Watching Blake get spanked was a huge turn on. But watching him get fucked...she couldn't think of anything hotter. And now that he was her true, collared slave, it was time to remind him of his place, just as Tom would take Sandy back home and remind her that when she was with him, she was submissive to him.

"Sandy," she said, "Will you help position Blake on the bed for me, face down? I want to tie his hands to the bedposts."

Sandy stopped the spanking. "Boo. Alright, up up," she said, and Blake got up off her lap. "No rubbing!" she warned, and Blake smiled, probably because Victoria always warned him against rubbing his bottom after a spanking. She wanted the spanking to hurt for as long as possible.

Blake lay over the edge of the bed, his feet on the floor and his freshly reddened bottom in the air. Sandy took one of his hands and secured it to one of the bedposts at the foot of the bed with the Velcro straps Victoria kept handy for just such an occasion.

Victoria tied his other hand to the opposite bedpost, creating the perfect vision of her slave, in bondage, recently punished, ass in the air, and about to get fucked by a very large Dom whether he knew it or not.

Victoria leaned over and whispered into Blake's ear. "Did you think I'd let you get out of being lent out to my friend here? You managed to win the wager last time, but now there's no wager to win. It's come down to a simple question. Are you willing to be my true slave? Are you willing to be my slut?"

Blake groaned. "Yes, Ma'am. I am willing."

Victoria didn't let him see her internal sigh of relief. She supposed she didn't need to get his permission, now that he'd already agreed to be her slave, since it involved a certain level of 'consensual non-consent'. But she liked to make him agree, each time, that he was doing this willingly. That he was agreeing to be fucked in the ass by a man for the very first time.

* * *

Blake's ass felt like it was on fire. Sandy had done a damn good job of beating his butt, that was for sure. She'd probably been lying over her own Master's knee and wishing she could find a man to whup. It was something he could kind of relate to. After all, fucking her hard had been fun, and it was something he couldn't really do to Victoria. No, Victoria liked to fuck *him* hard.

She'd used a strap-on on him before, which had the immediate effect of putting him into a deeply submissive mindset. It turned him on in a way he'd never thought possible. But to be fucked by a man? A fucking big ol' cowboy? Holy shit.

Behind him, he could hear Tom laughing that deep laugh of his.

"I sure hope you're ready for some cock," Tom said.

*Fuck.*

But he wanted to submit to Victoria, more than anything. He wanted to show her that he was completely hers, hers to do with as she pleased. And if it pleased her to tie him to her bed and let another man fuck his ass, then goddammit that's what he was going to do, even if it killed him.

Hopefully it wouldn't actually kill him. It was just a cock, right?

Tom spoke, and it seemed he was speaking to his slave girl. "Put the condom on me, darlin'. And plenty of lube. I'm gonna go easy on this one, at least at first." He laughed that laugh of his again, and Blake's stomach tightened in fear. Fear and...ah fuck, lust? His cock was hard again, pressing against the duvet insistently.

Suddenly Tom was behind him. Victoria sat on the bed, perhaps for a better view. She ran her fingers through Blake's hair and smiled at him. "What a good boy."

He felt Tom's large hands spread his ass cheeks, which still burned from Sandy's hand. Damn that girl had learned how to spank.

"Here we go," Tom said, and pressed the tip of his cock against Blake's tense asshole. He probed at it, pushing painfully forward, forcing Blake to open up to him.

The erotic pain of it made Blake's cock pulse with desire. When Tom thrust completely inside him, Blake screamed, unable to hold back. Victoria leaned over and gave him a tender kiss on his lips, something she rarely did, but tonight she'd done it twice. The sentiment was not lost on him.

She was pleased with him, happy he was taking it in the ass for her. For doing what she desired.

With that thought, the next thrust didn't hurt as much. Blake moaned as Tom moved in and out of him, and Blake's cock ground against the duvet, the friction nearly driving him over the edge. He was going to come, oh God.

"You like that?" Tom asked, still fucking him, harder than before. "You like when I fuck your sweet virgin ass?"

"Yes, Sir," he replied, before he even had a chance to think about it. It was true. He did like it, although he couldn't figure out why, exactly.

Then Tom's hand left his hip and reached around, grabbing Blake's painfully erect cock in his hand, and jerked it. Blake gasped, and within seconds he spurted all over the duvet. The ecstasy of his climax wasn't even tempered by the knowledge that Victoria would almost definitely make him clean up that mess on her duvet...with his tongue.

With a long grunt, Tom slammed into him once more and came, his cock emptying into the condom inside Blake's ass.

His ass pinched the moment Tom slipped out, and Blake moaned. He was no longer a virgin when it came to male-on-male sex. Kinda strange to think about, considering he never could have even imagined wanting that... until he met Victoria, and her methodical anal training had him practically begging for it now.

Tom laughed. "Damn, boy, that was some good fuckin'."

"Yes, Sir," Blake said. Victoria got off the bed, and unstrapped his hand from the bedpost. Blake couldn't see, perhaps she'd nodded to Sandy, because Sandy was untying his other hand.

"Stand up, little Blake," Victoria said.

He stood, feeling the burn deep inside him, and the tingle on his ass still. The purple duvet where his cock had been pressed was covered with his come. "I'm sorry, Ma'am," he said, heat rising in his cheeks.

"Well, don't be sorry, just take care of it. You know what to do."

Blake dropped to his knees and stuck his tongue out, ready to lap up his own come. Submitting to her this way wasn't easy in the beginning, but now he found himself doing it on a regular basis…and loving every second of it.

"Aww, Vicky," Tom said, and Blake raised his eyebrows. *Vicky?* "That was my fault. I gave your man-slut a bit of a reach-around."

Blake's cock twitched reflexively at the memory.

"Since it was my fault," Tom said, "My slave girl can do the clean up, now how's that sound?"

To his surprise, Victoria nodded. "Very well. Sandy, be sure to lick up every last drop. I want my duvet clean again."

Blake moved out of the way and sat back to watch, wincing as his ass touched the carpet. The sight of the beautiful blonde lapping up his come made his cock start to rise again, even though it had been only a few minutes since he last came.

"I love come, so this isn't bad for me," Sandy said merrily, and stuck her pink tongue out once more, licking the duvet in long strokes, cleaning up his mess.

Tom shook his head. "My girl is so hard to tame, sometimes, ain't you now, darlin'?"

Sandy nodded in agreement and grinned at her Dom, as if she knew what was coming.

"I think you should get your spanking here, instead of at home like I planned," Tom said.

Sandy blushed, but she kept licking at the duvet, even though Blake's come was all gone by now.

"Victoria," Tom said, "will you do the honors of punishing my slave for me?"

"I'd be happy to. Blake, you stay right where you are. I want you to watch and see what I look like when I'm paddling you."

Sandy looked nervous. "A paddle? Tom doesn't use a paddle on me."

"That's because Tom has big hard hands. I'm going to paddle you, and if you don't like it then you can ask your Dom for permission to bail out."

Sandy looked up at her Dom expectantly, with the look of a child who is used to getting every toy she asks for. "Please, Sir?"

He laughed, of course. Blake knew Tom would laugh at that.

"I think you could use a paddlin', sweetpea. Now you be a good girl and do what Miss Victoria says."

Sandy stood up and looked at Victoria expectantly.

Victoria looked so sexy, the way she stared Sandy down. That poor girl had no idea what she was in for. Victoria was a strict disciplinarian with a paddle, especially since she loved to play the governess.

"Well? What are you waiting for? Your Master won't save you, so lean over the desk and take your punishment."

Sandy looked nervous in earnest now, and she looked back at her Dom again briefly before obeying.

Her tan lines contrasted the pale globes of her ass with the tan of her legs, making her bottom look extremely appealing. Blake found himself wondering what that ass would look like reddened by his Mistress's paddle.

"I'm paddling you on behalf of your Master, Sandy," Victoria said ominously, and raised the paddle. "Consider this your maintenance." She brought the paddle down, and the resounding slap of wood on flesh filled the room, seeming to reverberate in his ears.

Sandy wailed, and kicked one slender foot up as if by instinct, then quickly lowered it.

Tom laughed. "Give her an extra one every time she kicks, if you'd be so kind. My girl needs to learn how to take a whuppin' properly."

"With pleasure." Victoria spanked her again with the paddle and Blake watched Sandy's feet with anticipation. Would she kick again?

No such luck. Apparently she could control herself if she really wanted to.

So many times he'd tried to control himself under Victoria's paddle only to find himself a whimpering, blubbering mess by the end, just the way his Mistress liked it. But that experience might be reserved just for him alone.

Sandy's ass turned bright red under Victoria's paddling, and a couple times she did end up kicking her foot up, just a little. The kick was always followed by a breathless "Sorry! Sorry!" which was followed by a quick extra smack right on her thigh, a move that stung like a bitch if Blake remembered correctly. How could he forget?

Is that what he looked like, hanging over the school desk that was situated in Victoria's room to help set the scene of their fantasies? Watching Sandy, he couldn't help but get turned-on at the thought. Her quivering thigh muscles, the jiggle of her ass when the paddle struck, the blotch of red color that popped up immediately...was that what happened when he was paddled?

Finally, after what seemed like a long time—and surely seemed even longer to Sandy—Victoria set the paddle down and helped Sandy stand up. Tears streaked her face, and her mascara had run. *Uh oh.* Had Victoria gone overboard with the punishment?

"Thank you, Miss Victoria," Sandy whispered, and to Blake's surprise—she hugged his Mistress, throwing her arms around her neck in a show of sincere gratitude. "I always feel so much more grounded after maintenance. That was... incredible." She took her Dom's hand and smiled up at him. "Thank you, too, Sir."

He gave her a peck on the lips, and the look of true love that coursed between them set off a flare of jealousy in Blake's gut. Would Victoria ever look at him that way? Did he want her to?

*Yes.* Yes, he did.

And he'd do anything to get her to look at him with the love of a Mistress for her slave.

Blake glanced over at Sandy. He wished he could be so gracious after a paddling like that. Instead, he had to be forced to say thank you, forced to kiss her paddle, despite his desire to show her his gratitude with the ease that Sandy had done so. Maybe with time he'd become better at being the perfect slave. But was that even in his nature?

Even now, he kept finding himself wondering what Victoria was up to when he wasn't around. How often did she go to BDSM clubs without him? A good slave wouldn't worry about that, probably. A good slave would just be happy to be well taken care of, and well punished.

Fuck.

It shouldn't bother him, but it did.

"We're goin' to head out now, darlin'," Tom said, giving Victoria a kiss on the cheek. "Thanks for lending me your slave's ass." He winked at Blake, and Blake couldn't help but to blush like a fucking school girl. If he hadn't had such an incredible orgasm maybe he'd be less embarrassed. Nah, probably not. The whole thing had turned him on, and whatever the hell that meant didn't even matter really, because it was Victoria he loved.

He loved her.

Maybe that was why he was feeling so territorial and jealous about the clubs?

And holy shit, he loved her.

Did she know? He looked over at his Mistress, who was leading Sandy and Tom to the door amidst promises to see them again soon. Blake smiled at them and followed behind Victoria like a puppy.

"Well," she said, turning to him after their guests had left. "That was fun, wasn't it?"

Blake kneeled on the floor in front of her, a position he knew she preferred he be in whenever possible. She smiled and ran her fingers through his hair, mussing it slightly.

"It was fun, Ma'am."

"Even the part where I lent you out to another man? Did you like that, little Blake?" She looked down at him, her curiosity evident in her eyes.

"Yes," he admitted. "I like being your slut, Ma'am."

She laughed. "I'm glad you enjoyed yourself."

Blake smiled but didn't respond. She seemed so happy now, he didn't want to ruin it by bringing up his concerns about her going to BDSM clubs without him. But how could he not? It would eat at him otherwise. He couldn't start their life together as her slave if he didn't even know where he stood when it came to other men.

"Ma'am, may I speak freely?"

\* \* \*

Victoria looked at him warily. He'd never asked that before. What was going on? "Go ahead."

"Thank you, Ma'am." He paused. "Can we sit on the couch, Ma'am?"

This was it. She'd pushed him too far, too fast. Now she'd have to let him go. That had to be what this was about. She could see it in his eyes. Was it because she pushed near the edges of his limits tonight? Was it because she asked him to submit to her in front of other people, when he was used to being dominated in complete privacy?

"Well, Blake," she said, sitting on one end of the leather couch. "You may sit here now, but as you know I prefer you on the floor, at my feet."

He sat next to her, and suddenly she was struck by his size, by how much bigger and taller he was than her. Normally that would turn her on—to relish how she could control a man who could easily overpower her if he wished—but now she felt like something was…different.

Something was going on. Where was her submissive little Blake?

He looked at her. "Ma'am, I want to bring something up and I want us to discuss it as... as equals. As a man and a woman in a relationship. Not as Mistress and slave."

Part of her wanted to refuse. To tell him it was her way or the highway, and that if he didn't want to be her slave then he should just leave.

The other part of her would die if he walked out that door.

"Go ahead."

Blake swallowed. "I want to be your slave. I really do. I want to serve you always. But..." He paused as if he was unsure of how to proceed.

"Go ahead—speak freely. I insist." She could feel her defenses rising in response to what she thought he might say. A huge part of her still held out hope that Blake was different. That he would be her soul mate and her slave, all in one. She'd had boyfriends in the past who wanted her to spank them in the bedroom but then wanted her to defer to them in everything else—but she wasn't the same woman now as she was back then. She'd grown, and her expectations for what a healthy relationship meant had also grown.

Now it seemed Blake was inching in the wrong direction for their relationship. Sitting on the couch next to her instead of kneeling by her feet. Telling her he wanted to speak as equals.

What he didn't get was that they already were equals—equal halves to the relationship, albeit with different responsibilities and duties. They were like yin and yang, the Domme and the sub. Neither could exist without the other. Didn't he get that?

"What's bothering you, Blake?" she asked, purposefully omitting her pet name for him by not referring to him as "little".

"I got the impression that you played with Tom and Sandy before," he blurted.

"Of course I have. They're old friends. I've known them longer than I've known you, certainly." She had a feeling she knew where this conversation was headed. Blake was jealous.

"Have you been going to BDSM clubs all this time?" he asked. "Without me?"

And there it was. She instinctively knew that Blake was letting his primal emotions overrun his good sense—that it was his jealousy talking. But she couldn't let her slave claim ownership over her, even if he already owned a bigger piece of her than she'd ever let on.

"Do you really want to be in charge of where I can and cannot go?" she asked coolly, hoping to keep the hurt out of her voice. "Is that how you want our relationship to be, with your Mistress accountable to you for her whereabouts?"

"Please," he said, taking her hand in his. "Just talk to me, for real, just for now."

"Okay, fine. You know how busy I am with work," she said. "Since I've met you, my free time has been taken up by you, mainly."

"Mainly." He said it with a tinge of sarcasm, and she shot him a stern look.

"Sorry, Ma'am," he murmured. Then, "But that sounds like yes, you've scened with other people. Without me."

"I have, yes. But it's something I've always done, and I didn't think you were ready to take your very confused submissive self out into the clubs, where other people would see you. Not when you're new to the BDSM community and lifestyle. Not when you weren't trained, either."

"You were afraid I'd embarrass you?" he asked.

"No, that's not what I meant." She sighed. "You wouldn't have felt comfortable there. Maybe you would now, but at the time, I didn't want to scare you off by taking you there when you weren't ready for it."

"But—" Blake kept his hand on hers, as if to ground himself. She let him because he looked like he needed to feel that connection to her. Couldn't blame him, really. She knew her body language had her half out the door already.

Blake spoke carefully. "I don't feel comfortable with you going to clubs without me. I don't like the idea of you having sex with other men or spanking them or letting them eat you out or any of the other things that I can't even imagine goes on there."

"No one has sex at the club," she said.

"Private parties, then."

"Sometimes at a private house, yes."

His jaw dropped. "So you admit you've cheated on me?"

This had gone far enough. "I don't like your tone, Blake. If you want to speak to me as my equal then don't relegate me to the role of naughty child. I won't have you scolding me. And no, I've never slept with anyone since we began seeing each other. But I have scened with other people at clubs, both men and women, like Sandy."

He looked heartbroken at her response.

"I'm sorry, Blake," she said softly. "I didn't know that would be a deal breaker for you."

Blake shook his head. "I'm upset, but we never discussed it before, I suppose. I know I have no right to say who you can and can't scene with—"

"We're discussing this as a couple," she reminded him. "As a man and a woman in a relationship."

"Yes, Ma'am."

"So let's set some boundaries."

He nodded. "Okay."

"Boundary number one: from now on, neither of us will play with anyone else, unless the other is present. That means if I want to go to a club, I'm taking you. If you want to be punished by someone else, I get to watch. Deal?"

"Deal, Ma'am," he said, smiling. "That would make me feel a lot better about everything, I think."

"Good. No more jealousy, then." She breathed a sigh of relief she hadn't even realized she was holding in. "Boundary number two: If you need to talk like this again, then let me know and we'll do it. But if you're rude to me, I reserve the right to punish you later for your lack of respect."

Blake paled. "I'm sorry, Ma'am. I didn't mean to get a disrespectful tone before." He got off the couch and sat by her feet, looking up at her. "I prefer the view from here, anyway."

She laughed. "Good." Seeing him on the floor made her horny again. Or maybe it was just the giddy feeling of relief that he wasn't breaking up with her, or telling her that he didn't want to be her slave after all. Thank goodness it wasn't that.

* * *

Blake smiled up at her, glad to be back on the floor, glad to be owned. He felt better knowing he hadn't ruined everything with his jealousy.

"As punishment for your tone earlier," she said, spreading her legs, "you'll be spending the next half-hour worshipping at my shrine."

"That's no punishment," he said. "I'm honored to do that for you, Ma'am."

"Hmm. True. Go get the mat, then."

Fuck. "Yes, Ma'am."

Blake got the welcome mat from the front door and set it on the carpet in front of where she sat on the couch with her legs spread. She grinned sadistically at him. Kneeling on the spiky plastic mat was going to be pure torture on his knees, but he relished the chance to prove to her once more that he really was hers to do with as she pleased.

"Ma'am?" he said, wincing as he kneeled on the mat. Victoria had laid her head back on the couch and closed her eyes, prepared to settle in for a nice long session with his tongue.

She opened her eyes. "Why are you still talking? Shouldn't your mouth be busy in other pursuits?"

Blake nodded and started to move her panties to the side before realizing she still wasn't wearing any. Nice.

He licked her labia, circling around her clit, flicking it gently with his tongue. His mouth was supposed to be busy, yes, but he had to tell her now before he lost his nerve. But…he'd already lost the nerve, a bit. So he kept his mouth on her clit as he murmured the words "I love you, Victoria." It came out sounding muffled.

She moaned, probably from the vibrations of his voice against her clit, then paused. "Wait, what did you just say?"

He lifted his face from her pussy and looked up at her. "I said, I love you, Victoria."

"Really?" She smiled that amazing smile of pure happiness she sometimes got on her face when he'd pleased her. It was that smile of hers that he worked so hard for. It made everything perfect.

His love for her pleased her, and that was awesome. He smiled and went back to licking her pussy, happy to see how wet she'd become from his ministrations.

"Blake, I'm so glad you're here with me," she whispered. "I'm so glad you're my slave."

"Thank you, Ma'am," he said, his lips against her pussy. Even his aching knees didn't ache so much when she said things like that.

"Get up," she ordered suddenly. "Go lie on the bed."

He started to crawl there but she jumped off the couch and swatted his ass. "No time to crawl, stand up and get your ass on the bed, please."

He laughed. No time? But he ran to the bed and jumped on just the same. The plush purple duvet was a welcome change on his skin compared to the hard plastic mat she'd had him on a moment ago.

She pushed him onto his back and straddled him, easily sliding his cock into her tight pussy. "This is where I like to be," she said, pumping herself up and down. "I like to ride my Blake pony."

"I'm yours," he said.

"Maybe I'll even make a horse's bit and saddle for my pony, what do you think about that?"

He grinned. She was constantly thinking up new ways to play, and he loved that so much about her. "I think I'd try really hard to be a good pony then, Ma'am."

"Good answer." She ground her hips against him, reaching up and squeezing one of her big pink nipples, tugging on it rhythmically as she rode herself into a frenzy.

With a gasp, her cunt tightened around him, and he breathed carefully, trying to hold off on coming until she was done. When she came, moaning loudly, he groaned and prayed she'd give him permission to come too.

"Yes, Blake, yes, come for me," she said, and he came inside her, pumping his hips as he emptied himself into her.

"We were in such a hurry we forgot the condom," she said, looking down in surprise.

*Oh shit.*

"Don't worry, we won't get pregnant," she assured him. "I'm on the Pill."

He nodded. Thank goodness. Although he wouldn't mind having kids someday, in the future. With her. He wanted to do everything with her.

"I love you," he said again. There was no fear of saying it now. He meant it.

She smiled and dropped down next to him, snuggling her body against his. "I love you too," she whispered. She laughed. "I've never said that before."

He pulled her against him and kissed her lips, something he rarely did because it didn't quite fit his role as her slave. Usually she was the one who decided when and where to kiss.

"Sorry, Ma'am," he apologized. "I just had the urge to kiss you when you said that."

"I'll allow it," she said. "In fact—do it again."

And he did.

*The End*

# BONUS!
## TAPE: AN EROTIC SHORT STORY

Carrie left her desk at five minutes to noon and went to the restroom to freshen up. She had to meet Mike down in the lobby soon so he could take her out to lunch for her birthday. It was very sweet of him to offer, especially since his hours were slightly different and their lunch breaks didn't always coincide.

She grabbed her coat and walked down the quiet hallway to the stairwell. The supply closet door was slightly ajar. Carrie frowned. Who was getting into the office supplies now? She knew for a fact that several of the interns were stealing envelopes and paperclips. And before the new receptionist started working there, she didn't have to reorder copy-paper nearly so often. Carrie sighed, walked over to the closet and pushed the door to close it, but it wouldn't budge.

*What on earth?*

Carrie opened the door to see what was blocking the way when a large, hard hand grabbed her by her upper arm and yanked her inside the closet, quickly closing the door behind her, leaving her shut in the dark with whoever was attached to that large hard hand.

She opened her mouth to scream but only a whimper came out. The darkness covered her like ice water and she groped wildly for the light switch, instead grazing a towering hulk of pure muscle.

*Oh no oh no oh no.*

Her captor turned her around, pressed her up against the door, and her heart beat so fast she was sure she'd die of a heart attack at any moment. But no, she was alive. And terrified. If she hadn't just emptied her bladder in the restroom, she would have pissed herself right then.

"Don't scream," he whispered. "Mike told me about your fantasy. And I'm gonna make it come true."

"No," she protested weakly, even as her mind worked in overdrive to figure out who had her pressed against the supply room door, her face pushed against the cool, paint-smelling beige wall. He was big and strong, and he knew Mike. She quickly dismissed the idea that it might be Mike himself—although Mike had a similar build—because Mike was so quiet and shy and had been that way ever since they started dating over six months ago. But who would Mike have told her most intimate secret to— that she wanted to be, well, taken? And taken... at work?

She cursed under her breath. She never should have told him that when she was drunk. She'd hoped that he'd forgotten, that perhaps he'd been drunk enough to forget. But of course not. Mike never got drunk. And now some idiot friend of his was going to fucking rape her.

"Are you okay?" the man asked, no longer whispering.

*Oh thank God.* It was Mike. The shock that the man who'd just pulled her into the supply room was her shy boyfriend after all was quickly replaced with relief. Then anger.

She started to turn around, to smack his arm, to tell him he scared her half to death—but he held her face against the wall and said, very softly, "Yes, it's me. If you want me to stop, tell me now. But if you stay silent, I'm going to fuck the shit out of you right here."

Oh God, she couldn't. She shouldn't. But this was her fantasy come true. How could she not?

Her silence while she thought the matter through was apparently enough to imply consent to Mike, because before she had even fully decided that she was actually going to do this, Mike grabbed her wrists.

"Do as I say and you won't get hurt," he said. A line right out of her own fantasy. But in her fantasy...

The sound of packing tape being roughly torn off the tape gun interrupted her thought. Yes, that was it. The tape. Just the thought of it, the sound of it, of—God the feel of it—as he wrapped it around her wrists, keeping them behind her back, made her wet. She struggled, to feel what it would finally feel like to struggle against tape, and was rewarded with a smack on her ass harder than she'd ever have thought Mike would hit her. He'd never shown her before what six feet of pure male muscle actually meant—that a spanking from him would actually hurt. Her panties dampened again with arousal.

Behind her, Mike breathed raggedly as he pressed himself against her. His erection strained through his pants and prodded her ass.

"Fuck me," she whispered, and he smacked her ass again, pushing her against the wall completely, so that her breasts, still fully clothed in an underwire bra and silk blouse, pressed up against the plasterboard.

"You don't speak or I'll use this fucking tape as a gag. Nod if you understand."

She nodded, equal parts terrified and turned on. Mike never cursed. He never would do this sort of thing—the sort of thing she masturbated to the thought of. Except...it was happening.

Her mind raced. She couldn't talk? Or should she, just to get the punishment of the gag? No, that would hurt too much—the packing tape on her lips. She'd certainly get exfoliated, that was for sure. Possibly waxed. He fumbled with her button and fly, and she moved to help him but couldn't, not with her hands taped firmly behind her back. The feel of the bondage was so perfect, so real.

*'Cause it is real. I'm tied up, and I'm at this strange new Mike's mercy.*

"Are you wet for me, birthday girl?" Mike asked, letting her pants drop unceremoniously to the floor.

She moaned, nodded, her forehead rubbing against the wall. She was so wet.

He pulled down her underwear—plain cotton—and slid his fingers between her thighs, running them across her labia, purposefully—or so she imagined—skipping her clit, leaving her squirming and desperate for more contact. The sound of his zipper opening made her even wetter, and she wriggled her hips as much as she could while sandwiched between the wall and his muscular torso. His cock pressed against her naked buttocks, the tip leaving a cold trail of pre-cum across her skin. It felt sticky and dirty and oh so perfect.

"Fuck me," she whispered again, and gasped since she hadn't meant to speak, hadn't meant to—the sound of a piece of tape coming off the tape dispenser sent shivers running down her spine.

"Please—" she said, her words cut off by the clear tape over her mouth. His large, warm hand came around to her face and pressed the tape gag down firmly, briefly touching her nostrils. *He's making sure I can breathe*, she realized.

"Now shut the fuck up," he said, and her pussy clenched. "Are you ready?"

She nodded again as best she could, and he slammed into her so hard she couldn't hold back her moans of ecstasy tinged with erotic pain. He hit her g-spot, and he thrust in again, making her pussy take him eagerly. He was a big guy, and had the cock to match. It was actually a bit too big for her, though, and a lot of their time in bed was spent in positions where he could gently slide just half of it into her, and let the other half slide through her legs. That way he got the friction and she didn't have to deal with getting her cervix bruised. He was thoughtful like that.

But this Mike—the office supply closet Mike—didn't seem to care if he hurt her. And it was because he knew that's what she wanted, what she craved.

*Fuck me hard*, she thought, wishing she could say it, but grateful for the feel of the tape on her lips to prevent her. Because if he fucked her as hard as he could…she couldn't even imagine what that would feel like.

*I'm about to find out.*

His cock stroked deep inside of her, deeper than it had gone before other than accidentally, until it nudged against her womb and made her cry out, her sounds muffled by the tape.

"You're gonna take all of my cock, slut," he whispered, his breath hot on her ear. "You're gonna take it and you're gonna like it."

*Oh God yes.* She did like it. Her pussy was stretched wide from his thickness, and he hit spots that she never even knew existed. Everything seemed to swell inside her as her pussy swallowed his cock, and she moaned when he poked her cervix again and again, eliciting an exquisite pain deep within her. It was something she'd never felt before. He'd never fucked her this hard.

She tried to move her hips to meet his thrusts, but his hand came around her hip, and he played with her clit from the front. The sensation was overwhelming and she squirmed against his hand, only succeeding in making him thumb her clit faster, until she was breathing hard through her nose and moaning against the tape with pleasure. Her climax crested and she came, covering his hand and still-pounding cock with her fluids.

He growled as if in appreciation behind her and slammed into her once, twice, and then he came inside of her, his come filling her and dripping out down the insides of her naked thighs.

His head rested on the wall next to hers, his chest pressed against her back, the little buttons on his shirt rubbing against her bound hands. He stayed there until his heartbeat, which she could feel thudding against her back, slowed.

The pressure of his warm body against hers was gone suddenly when he stepped away from her. She heard him pull up his own pants and zip the fly.

"Maybe I should leave you like this," he said softly. "All taped up and gagged, with your pants down around your ankles and cum running down your legs."

Imagining that happening, imagining getting caught—she moaned in excitement, and he laughed.

"You'd like that, wouldn't you, slut?" he asked, and reached back around to feel her cunt. He played with her clit again and she protested weakly against the tape covering her mouth. Her post-orgasmic pussy was too sensitive for more stimulation. But Mike knew that about her. It was this new, office-supply closet Mike who didn't care if she didn't think she could handle another orgasm. His hand flicked her clit faster, not relenting until she came again, her nostrils flaring over the tape gag with the exertion.

"This might hurt," he advised, and he held the corner of the tape that was pressed against her lips with his fingers, which smelled like sex.

*Oh God this was going to really hurt.* She winced in expectation of a quick yank that would pull the skin off of her face, but Mike took his time and carefully pulled the tape off.

"Thank you," she said, and moved her hands to touch her tingling lips, once again forgetting they were taped up behind her.

"Let me get a scissor," he said behind her, and he switched on the light, bathing them in the fluorescent glare. "Don't move, I don't want to cut you."

He freed her hands and she turned around to face him, finally. Yes, it was Mike, but he was different somehow. He looked stronger, more in charge. Sexier.

"That was hot," he said, grinning. He bent down and helped her pull up her pants. "I'd like to do it again sometime."

"Yes!" she replied, not even trying to play it cool. "I'd love that."

"But next time, I get to choose when and where."

*Oh my God.* The thought made her weak in the knees. And wet.

"So wherever you go, from now on, whenever you go out on your errands, or even if you're just going to sleep in your own house—you'll never know when I might just…take you. And tape you up."

With that, Mike grabbed the packing tape. "I'm stealing this."

*The End.*

# ABOUT SHOSHANNA EVERS

*New York Times* and *USA Today* Bestselling author Shoshanna Evers has written dozens of sexy stories, including The Man Who Holds the Whip (part of the bestselling MAKE ME anthology), Overheated, The Enslaved Trilogy, and The Pulse Trilogy (from Simon & Schuster Pocket Star).

Her work has been featured in Best Bondage Erotica 2012 and Best Bondage Erotica 2013, the Penguin/Berkley Heat anthology Agony/Ecstasy, and numerous erotic BDSM novellas including Chastity Belt and Punishing the Art Thief from Ellora's Cave Publishing.

The non-fiction anthology Shoshanna Evers edited and contributed to, How To Write Hot Sex: Tips from Multi-Published Erotic Romance Authors, is a #1 Bestseller in the Authorship, Erotica Writing Reference, and Romance Writing categories.

Shoshanna is also the cofounder of **SelfPubBookCovers.com**, the largest selection of one-of-a-kind, premade book covers in the world.

Shoshanna is a New York native who now lives with her family and three big dogs in Northern Idaho. She welcomes emails from readers and writers, and loves to interact on Twitter and Facebook.

*Sexily \*Evers\* After...* **ShoshannaEvers.com**

# SHOSHANNA EVERS WANTS YOU TO STAY IN TOUCH!

Website: ShoshannaEvers.com
Newsletter (right side of the page!):
   ShoshannaEvers.com/blog
Blog: TheWritersChallenge.com
Twitter: Twitter.com/ShoshannaEvers
Facebook: Facebook.com/Shoshanna.Evers
Goodreads: goodreads.com/shoshannaevers
Email: shoshannaevers@gmail.com


****To my readers: If you enjoyed this book, I'd love if you could leave an honest review! Reviews are so important, thank you for taking the time—I really appreciate it!

ISBN-10: 0991372247
ISBN-13: 978-0-9913722-4-9

# Shoshanna
# EVERS

ShoshannaEvers.com